Socce

Jon wanted to take this k

Luke saw the glint in
knew he meant business. The foul had riled him.

'The Harriers may live to regret what they've just done,' murmured the commentary, sotto voce for a change, so as not to forewarn the opposition. 'They've just woken up Jon Crawford, the Swifts' multi-talented guest star...'

## Soccer Shocks

'Hey! What's got into you, Tubs?' Gregg shouted. 'Where's the fire?'

It was some while before Tubs was in any state to answer. He looked shocked as well as out of breath. 'At the . . . recky!' he gasped, heaving.

'What d'yer mean, at the recky? What is?'

'The fire . . . you idiot!'

'What fire?' demanded Luke, suddenly concerned.

'The fire . . . that burnt down . . . the cabin!'

# ROB CHILDS

# SOCCER STARS COLLECTION

### including
### SOCCER STARS and SOCCER SHOCKS

### Illustrated by
### JON RILEY

## CORGI YEARLING BOOKS

SOCCER STARS COLLECTION
A CORGI YEARLING BOOK: 978 0 440 86590 2 (from January 2006)
0440 86590 5

This collection first published 2003
Copyright © Rob Childs, 2003

3 5 7 9 10 8 6 4

including

SOCCER STARS
First published in Great Britain by Corgi Yearling Books, 1999
Text copyright © Rob Childs, 1999
Illustrations copyright © Jon Riley, 1999

SOCCER SHOCKS
First published in Great Britain by Corgi Yearling Books, 2001
Text copyright © Rob Childs, 2001
Illustrations copyright © Jon Riley, 2001

Set in 12/15 pt New Century Schoolbook

Young Corgi Books are published by Random House Children's Books,
61-63 Uxbridge Road, London W5 5SA,
a division of The Random House Group Ltd,
in Australia by Random House Australia (Pty) Ltd,
20 Alfred Street, Milsons Point, Sydney, NSW 2061, Australia,
in New Zealand by Random House New Zealand Ltd,
18 Poland Road, Glenfield, Auckland 10, New Zealand,
and in South Africa by Random House (Pty) Ltd,
Isle of Houghton, Corner of Boundary Road & Carse O'Gowrie,
Houghton 2198, South Africa.

THE RANDOM HOUSE GROUP Limited Reg. No. 954009
www.kidsatrandomhouse.co.uk

A CIP catalogue record for this book is available from the British Library.

Printed and bound in Great Britain by
Cox & Wyman Ltd, Reading, Berkshire

# ROB CHILDS

# SOCCER STARS

**Illustrated by Jon Riley**

Corgi Yearling Books

*For all budding young soccer stars*

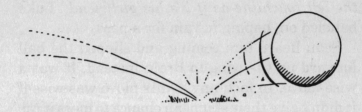

# 1 Sick as a Parrot

*'The Swifts are on the attack again, inspired by the half-time pep talk from their player-manager, Luke Crawford. This is the last league game before Easter and we must . . . er, I mean, they must get a result today . . .'*

It wasn't easy for the commentator to remain neutral. He was so involved in the match that he was actually playing in it as well.

Doing a running commentary was just one of Luke's many self-appointed roles for Swillsby Swifts. Besides being player-manager, he captained and coached the Under-13 Sunday

League side too. It was *his* team. He had formed it and signed up all the players. About the only thing he steered well clear of was washing their gold strip. He left that job to his mum.

'*The elegant Sean has the ball now, hugging the left touchline as if it's his girlfriend,*' Luke babbled on, hoping in vain for a pass.

Sean heard him coming and slipped the ball forward up the wing to Brain instead. It was a wise move. In fact, any Swifts move was wise if it didn't give their skipper a chance to mess it up. It was an unwritten club rule that would never be posted up on the changing cabin wall alongside many others: DON'T PASS TO LUKE.

'*The tricky winger takes on two defenders and weaves past both of them – super skills!*' continued the breathless commentary, undeterred. '*Brain cuts inside into the penalty area . . . it looks like he's going to shoot . . .*'

Brain had already shot while the words were still tumbling out of Luke's mouth. The Swifts' leading scorer was deadly with either foot and he unleashed a terrific strike with his right. The keeper only dived on top of the ball as it was bouncing back from the net.

'*GOOOAAALLL!!! The equalizer! Brain's done it again!*'

Luke's shriek of delight was a cue for the team celebrations to start. Players arrived from all over the pitch to mob the scorer and make fools of themselves in a wild war dance. Goals were something of a rare luxury for the Swifts and the boys liked to make the most of them.

'Great goal!' whooped Gary, their left wing-back, when they had finally calmed down a little. 'How many's that you've got now?'

Brain gave a shrug. 'Dunno. You'd better ask Luke.'

The skipper was bound to know. The details of every match were crammed into his notebook of soccer statistics. He kept a record of all the school games too in another book, even though his own appearances for Swillsby Comprehensive were few and far between. Luke didn't pick the Comp team.

'We've got 'em on the run,' he called out, shaking his fists to urge his teammates to greater efforts. 'C'mon, men, we can win this game now.'

'What's he going on about up there?' drawled Sanjay from his goal. 'Can't hear him.'

'You're not missing anything,' said Tubs, the Swifts' roly-poly full-back. 'Just the skipper's usual drivel.'

'Yeah, I know that. It's just that I'm collecting examples of his best drivel. I'm thinking of doing a piece on them for the school magazine. Should be a good laugh.'

'Concentrate!' Luke shouted. 'It's criminal to give away a soft goal straight after you've scored. You can get locked up for less than that.'

'There's another for my article,' Sanjay smirked. 'He's the one who ought to be locked up – for trying to play football while the balance of his mind is disturbed.'

'We know he's mad,' Tubs guffawed. 'Soccer mad!'

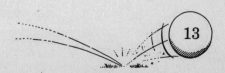

13

'Yeah, trouble is, I reckon we might all be getting as crazy as he is.'

The match was now level at 1–1, but the mood had swung in favour of the Swifts – and so had the blustery March wind. Its increasing strength helped to pin the visitors, Leeford Lions, in their own half.

*'The Lions have lost their roar and are playing like lambs,'* warbled the broadcaster in the number nine shirt. *'Every dog has his day, as they say, and the Swifts have got their tails up, sniffing the scent of the fox. These big cats are fast running out of lives . . .'*

Luke was in danger of running out of animals too as his cliché-ridden commentary became ever more bizarre. He'd already worked in allusions to giraffe-necks, tortoise shells, slippery eels and charging rhinoceros. As Tubs sent a hefty clearance upfield, Luke treated anyone within reception range to another four-legged simile. This time he likened their pacy right-winger to *'a greyhound springing out of its trap after the hare'*.

It was only because Dazza was the 100 metre sprint champion in his year group that he managed to catch the windswept ball and keep it in play near the corner flag. The slow full-back

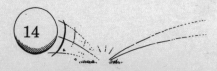

had long given up such an unequal contest and Dazza found himself with only the Lions goalie for company.

Dazza did what he always did when he had the ball at his feet and time to think what to do with it. He panicked. Instead of dribbling nearer, he lashed the ball vaguely goalwards, slicing across it with the outside of his boot. The ball swerved and swirled in the wind, curling out of the keeper's reach into the top far corner of the net.

'One in a million!' cried Luke. 'A real stunner, Dazza. Bet you couldn't do that again if you tried.'

The skipper was probably right for once. Dazza could have spent the next few years practising the other 999,999 times without repeating his success.

As commentator, however, Luke was temporarily lost for words. He couldn't conjure up any creature that would quite serve to describe the wobbly flight path of such a fluke shot. He was just happy to join in the impromptu party hosted by the lucky lottery winner.

It was all too much. His previous warning about gift goals went unheeded. Mentally, the Swifts were still counting the unexpected riches of three points when the Lions carved through their non-existent defence to score an instant equalizer. Sanjay ruefully picked the ball out of the net, the first Swifts' player to touch it since Dazza's boomerang.

'I don't believe it!' sighed Luke. 'That was just so sloppy.'

'Never mind, skipper,' said Brain. 'We can always hope for another miracle.'

'Yeah, the Swifts winning would be a miracle,' said Gregg, Gary's identical twin. 'I can't remember what it feels like.'

To their credit, the Swifts did try their best to recover from the setback. But, as usual, their

best wasn't good enough. The goal had put the Lions back on top and, despite the gale, they gave Sanjay – and Tubs – several uncomfortable moments before the final whistle.

The Swifts survived by the width of a goalpost, the length of Sanjay's outstretched leg and then the ample dimensions of Tubs's midriff bulge. Leaning against the creaking post at a corner, Tubs took a shot full in the stomach and he doubled up on the line.

'Lost ball!' cried Gary. 'It's disappeared in Tubs's flab.'

As the referee blew for full-time, perhaps not wishing to go and search for the ball, the Swifts gathered around their winded, last-second saviour.

'Worth it, Tubs,' said Luke, failing to show too much sympathy. 'Saved a certain goal, that did, and let us hang on for a vital point.'

The defender's podgy face began to turn a delicate shade of green as Luke rambled on regardless. 'Shows how much we've improved this season, men. The Lions beat us 5–0 at their place before Christmas. Now we've got a draw against them. Bet they're feeling as sick as parrots right now . . .'

Tubs rolled over and noisily deposited the half-digested remains of his large lunch into Sanjay's upturned goalie cap that he kept behind the post.

'They're not the only ones,' murmured the goalkeeper in dismay.

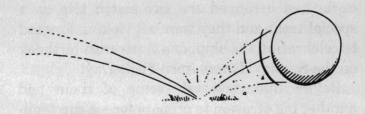

## 2   Home and Away

'Not wearing your cap, Sanjay?'

'Can I borrow it a minute? We've got a maths test after break.'

Sanjay had half-expected such attempts at coarse humour from his mates when he arrived at school next day. He ignored them and glanced at Tubs. 'Noticed you didn't offer to take the cap home and clean it up yourself.'

'Yeah, I'm fine now, thanks for asking,' Tubs replied sarcastically. 'Not my fault your stupid cap was lying there. I didn't do it on purpose.'

'Wouldn't put it past you.'

Aside from the contents of Sanjay's cap, there were two other main topics of conversation during the last week of term. The most important one for the Swifts was the exciting prospect of going away on a weekend tour. Luke's dad and uncle had arranged the two-match trip as a special treat and they were all looking forward to celebrating the skipper's thirteenth birthday on the Sunday. It was April Fools Day!

Before that, however, some of them had another big occasion to prepare for – a cup semi-final for the school on Thursday afternoon. Swillsby Comprehensive's grumpy sports teacher, 'Frosty' Winter, had relied heavily on one simple tactic in steering his limited Year 8 squad through the early rounds of the competition. It basically boiled down to not having too many Swifts in the team, and especially not Luke Crawford.

His small pool of players meant that certain choices were often forced upon him. Sanjay, for instance, was the only recognized goalkeeper in the year group, even though the likeness was somewhat tenuous. And speaking of likenesses, the reason both the Garner twins were regulars for the Comp was that Frosty still couldn't tell them apart.

He only had himself to blame for the shortage of available talent. His notorious short fuse and lashing tongue had driven several of the better footballers away. Much to the teacher's chagrin, Luke appeared to be immune to the effects of *Frostbite*, as they called it.

The boy's passion for the game meant that all Frosty's best efforts to humiliate and ridicule him had failed to work. Even attempted murder in the changing room would be unlikely to make Luke miss a practice session. It might only delay his arrival for a few minutes while he wriggled free of the rope that suspended him from the shower fittings.

Luke was the first one in the training grids as usual at the start of Tuesday's practice. He dribbled a ball around inside one of the square grids by himself, feigning to sell dummies to invisible opponents. More often than not, his quick turns left him on his backside when his feet became clumsily entangled.

'*And here we see Luke Crawford sharpening up his skills for the Swifts' Easter tour . . .*' burbled the commentary softly. Luke had spotted some of the others approaching and lowered the volume, '*. . . he shields the ball cleverly with his body, then throws his opponent off-balance with*

*a sudden twist and darts away . . . oops!'*

'What yer doing, sitting in the mud, Luke?' Gary called out.

'Just having a rest, waiting for you lot,' he replied casually. 'What's kept you?'

'Frosty's been sorting out transport and stuff with us for Thursday.'

'I didn't know he was going to be doing that.'

The players glanced at each other and smirked. 'No, I think he waited till you'd dashed out the changing room,' Gregg confessed. 'You know what he's like.'

Luke sighed and scrambled to his feet. 'Has the team been announced?' he asked, trying to keep any note of hope out of his voice. He was almost resigned to missing out on the semi-final. He hadn't played for the Comp for weeks, not even as a substitute.

His cousin Jon, the Comp's star striker and captain, answered. 'Soz, Luke, 'fraid there's no place for you. I did put in a good word, but . . .'

'Yeah, I know, Johan, thanks. C'mon, you can have some shooting practice at me in goal before Frosty gets here and spoils things.'

Luke loved watching his cousin in action. Jon's enviable ball skills seemed to come so naturally to him, just as they once did to Johan Cruyff, the most gifted player in the star-studded Dutch team of the 1970s. It was little wonder that Luke had nicknamed Jon after his all-time soccer hero.

If Jon was poetry in motion on the football field, Luke in comparison was more like a tedious comprehension exercise. But he was still hugging himself at his own recent stroke of genius. He had persuaded Jon to desert his crack Sunday League side this weekend and 'guest' for the Swifts on tour. The Padley Panthers had reluctantly given their consent, provided that

Jon only played on one of the days.

'You looking forward to the tour, Johan?' asked Luke after he retrieved one of his shots from the tangled netting.

'Sure,' came back the reply. 'Should be great fun.'

'Yeah, but it's serious, too, you know. I'd like to win both matches. Winning's a good habit for a team. It'll help us in our crucial league games after Easter. You want to play Saturday or Sunday?'

'Up to you, Luke . . . or is that Skipper?' grinned Jon, referring to his cousin's preferred term of address on Swifts' duty. 'I'll play in whichever game you think I'm most needed. You're the boss.'

That was sweet music to Luke's ears. He just wished the others might be so respectful. Frosty certainly wasn't when he appeared on the scene.

'Right, you lot, let's get cracking. No time to mess around in these grids. I want to practise some corners. Brain, you take them from both sides. Luke, you act as ball boy behind the goal . . .'

Luke didn't bother travelling to watch the semi-final. He would get all the details from Jon later. He had better things to do with his time – like deciding on tactics and formations for the Swifts' two tour matches.

As soon as he arrived home from school, he went up to his bedroom and switched on the computer. He needed to finish off compiling the tour dossier and print out a copy for each member of the squad. It would normally have been a totally absorbing labour of love, but he found it strangely difficult to concentrate. His mind kept straying on to the Comp's cup-tie.

'Wonder what's happening?' he murmured, checking the time again. 'Should be well into the second half by now. Hope we make the Final. Quite fancy playing in that and winning a medal . . .'

At that very moment, the Comp were desperately clinging on to a 1–0 lead, given to them by Gregg on the stroke of half-time. He'd scrambled the ball over the line after the goalkeeper had parried a shot from Brain, the one Swifts' player that Frosty was glad to have in his side.

'C'mon, ref, blow that whistle,' the teacher urged, jabbing at his watch. 'Time's up.'

It was wishful thinking. There were still several minutes to go and Frosty doubted whether the Comp could hold out for much longer. Their goal had been under almost constant pressure throughout the second period, but somehow remained intact. Sanjay was having one of his better – or luckier – days.

'Here they come again,' the goalkeeper cried as the home team launched yet another attack in search of the equalizer. 'Mark up tight, defence.'

The winger slipped the ball through Gary's legs and thumped over a high centre to the far post where the number ten was lurking, completely unmarked. Sanjay might as well have saved his breath, but at least he did manage to save the header. He leapt across his goal in spectacular fashion and plucked the ball out of the air with both hands.

'Boot it right away upfield,' yelled Frosty. 'Anywhere will do. Just get rid of the thing.'

Sanjay was annoyed at the lack of praise and threw the ball out instead to Big Ben, the gangly Swifts' centre-back who had come on as a substitute. Big Ben wasn't expecting it and Sanjay's warning shout came too late to prevent the loose ball from being collected by an attacker.

With Sanjay out of position, the goal was at his mercy. The boy was so certain he was going to score that he delayed his shot, savouring the moment. All he had to do was roll . . .

No-one quite knew where Gary came from, or how he got there in time. One second Frosty was cursing, the next he was astonished to see the

ball whipped off the striker's toes by Gary's last-ditch sliding tackle.

The groans of disappointment from the home supporters soon turned to howls of dismay. Brain had broken away up the left wing and pierced the defence with a through pass to Jon who supplied the *coup de grâce*. The ball was struck first time, on the run, and snaked low into the bottom corner of the net.

Instead of facing a replay, the Comp were now 2–0 up and the match was as good as over. They had booked their place in the Final.

It was a rare smile indeed that began to creep across the unfamiliar territory of Frosty's stubbled face. Not knowing which way to go, it soon lost its nerve and quickly disappeared. Jon thought he might just have seen it, but put it down to a trick of the light.

That really would have been something to tell Luke to record in his little black book. *The day that Frosty smiled.* Jon reckoned his cousin might have had more difficulty in believing that than the actual scoreline.

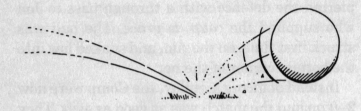

## 3   On Tour

'Typical!' grumbled Sanjay. 'Didn't take long for things to go wrong.'

'Yeah, at least it normally waits till after we kick off,' said Sean.

The goalkeeper sighed. 'We'll be lucky if the whole tour isn't jinxed, with you-know-who helping to organize it.'

'Might even have to be called off at this rate.'

'Oh, don't say that!' cried Brain. 'We've all been looking forward to this trip for weeks. Y'know, going off on tour like real footballers do.'

'Well, guess this is just about as close as most

of us will ever get to being *real* footballers,' grunted Tubs, looking around them. 'Sitting on a pavement kerb in Padley, five miles from home.'

The Swifts had stopped to pick up Luke's Italian cousin, Ricki, and their hired minibus clearly didn't fancy the rest of the journey. As they tried to set off again, the engine had stuttered, whined and died.

'I thought this old crate had complained a bit when Tubs climbed on board,' remarked Gary.

'Can't say I blame it,' put in his twin. 'And then adding another Crawford was just too much for it.'

'I am not a Crawford,' Ricki protested. 'My name is Fortuna.'

'Yeah, yeah, we know that, Ricki,' said Gregg. 'But you're half a Crawford. You can't help it if your mum comes from a disaster-prone family. They've got the *Sadim* touch.'

'Sadim?'

'That's Midas in reverse. Everything they touch turns to dross!'

'Like the Swifts,' muttered Big Ben. 'Having four and a half Crawfords on this tour was just asking for trouble.'

'Hey, I heard that,' Jon butted in, grinning.

'Soz, Jon, you must be the exception. You *have* got the golden touch!'

Luke and his dad had gone off with Jon's dad to the hire company in town to seek a replacement vehicle. Uncle Ray's large estate car was also being used to ease the overcrowding on the bus, with luggage stuffed into the back and strapped on to the roofrack.

'They went plenty time ago,' said Ricki. 'We will be late for kick-off s'afto.'

'Your English is getting better than mine,' said Tubs. 'When are you off back to sunny Italy?'

'Soon, I think. We only came for few months, y'know.'

'You'll still be here after Easter, won't you?'

'I hope so. Plenty important games to play, yes?'

'Dead right, there, Ricki,' said Big Ben. 'Luke won't let you out of the country till the end of the season. He still believes we can avoid finishing bottom of the league.'

'Perhaps we wouldn't be in the mess we are if you'd been able to play for us more often,' said Sanjay. 'Not seen you for ages.'

Ricki shrugged and spread his hands. 'My father, he wants me to play rugby on Sundays.

Is difficult, y'know, but rugby is over now. I am free as . . . how you say . . . a budgie.'

'Yeah, close. Something like that,' the goal-keeper replied and then jumped to his feet. 'Hey! Look, they've got a new bus.'

Judging by its appearance, not to mention the registration plate, the 'new' minibus was even older than the original.

'Huh! No expense spared, I see, Skipper,' said Tubs as Luke clambered out of the creaking back door. 'Not exactly the latest model, is it?'

Luke pulled a face. 'This was all they'd got left on a Saturday morning so don't knock it.'

'I wouldn't dare. Things might drop off.'

'We haven't got time to hang around while they fix the first one. It was either this or nothing.'

Tubs eyed the bus suspiciously. 'I think you made the wrong choice.'

There was a stampede for any spare places in Ray's car before the boys reluctantly began to reload their belongings into the bus. They were reassured to find that at least it was fitted with seat belts.

'Sorry about the delay,' said Philip, Luke's dad, clasping himself into the driver's seat. 'Next stop, Tibworth, for our first match.'

'Next stop, lunch, I hope,' said Tubs. 'I'm starving.'

Ray's packed estate car led the minibus along the tree-lined drive through the grounds of Tibworth Manor.

'Cool!' breathed Jon. 'Is this where Tibworth All Stars play?'

The country mansion at last came into view and his dad grinned. 'Bit grander than Swillsby recky, eh? The chap who runs the All Stars owns this place. He was a pro footballer himself once, apparently.'

'Sounds like we might need you today, Jon,' said Sean.

''Fraid not. Luke's decided to save me till tomorrow.'

'That's crazy!' protested Mark, Big Ben's partner in central defence.

'That's Luke for you!' agreed Sean, giggling.

As the vehicles scrunched to a halt in the gravelled car park, a man came out of the house. He strode towards them, limping slightly, his grim face showing no intention of offering hospitality to the travellers.

'My name's Miller – coach of the All Stars,' he called out brusquely as the two drivers emerged. 'Almost given you lot up.'

'Sorry we're late,' replied Philip Crawford. 'Had a breakdown.'

Sanjay couldn't resist making a loud comment from the rear of the bus. 'Yeah, a mental one, putting up with us all season.'

The coach did not seem to appreciate the joke. 'Tell yer players to get a move on. I'm a busy man. I just hope you're worth the wait.'

'Nice bloke,' muttered Ray as the coach turned away.

Luke had been studying him carefully. 'Sure I've seen that guy somewhere before. What did he say his name was?'

'Miller, I think,' said Gary. 'C'mon, let's go and get changed. I'm in a hurry too. I'm desperate for the toilet.'

As everyone piled out of the minibus, Luke was still preoccupied over the puzzle. Then, in the distance, he saw the coach kick some practice balls onto the pitch and the penny suddenly dropped. And so did his jaw.

'Of course – Robbie Miller!'

'Who's Robbie Miller when he's at home?' asked Tubs.

Mark overheard him. 'He *is* at home. This is his front garden!'

'You must have heard of Robbie Miller!' Luke exclaimed.

The Swifts looked at him blankly. Even his dad and uncle admitted that the name didn't mean much to them. Luke could scarcely believe it.

'Robbie Miller was only one of Scotland's greatest players back in the Sixties,' he stated. 'Along with people like Denis Law and Jim Baxter.'

'Oh, I've heard of them all right,' said Dad. 'Brilliant, they were.'

'So was Robbie Miller. Well, till he broke his leg, anyway, playing in the F.A. Cup Final one year. I've got loads of pictures of him in my old soccer annuals. Must get his autograph.'

Sanjay laughed. 'You're a mine of useless information, Skipper. I've no idea how you remember every little detail like you do. Bet you know more about his career than he does.'

'Don't encourage him,' groaned Tubs. 'We'll be here all day.'

Gary couldn't bear the thought of that. He was off, wriggling his way towards the changing rooms. When the rest of the squad reached there, they discovered that their skipper's memory was

not infallible. He had forgotten his football boots.

Luke was mortified. 'Must've left them in that other bus,' he wailed. 'What am I gonna do? I can't play in trainers.'

'You can borrow mine,' Jon offered. 'We take the same size.'

'Really? Your boots!' cried Luke in amazement. 'Don't you mind?'

Jon laughed. 'Why should I? There's nothing special about them.'

'It's what's inside the boots that counts,' said

Uncle Ray proudly. 'Perhaps Jon's goal-scoring magic will rub off on you today, Luke, eh?'

The first thing Luke did in Jon's boots was to win the toss. 'A lucky omen,' he murmured and then switched into commentary mode.

*'The Swifts' skipper, Luke Crawford, has decided to kick towards the manor in the first half, hoping to use the wind. He wants his team to make a good impression in this opening match of their tour. Especially now in front of the great Robbie Miller. A good start is so important . . .'*

The All Stars obviously agreed. After five minutes, Luke's borrowed boots had only had one kick each, and that was to restart the game. Sanjay had touched the ball just twice too, performing his regular job of fishing the ball out of the back of his net.

The Swifts' hapless goalkeeper was good at doing that. He'd had lots of practice all season.

# 4    Star-struck

By half-time, the Swifts were 7–0 down.

Luke was about to launch into his usual frantic team talk when Robbie Miller trudged past. 'You lot aren't fit to play on here,' he snarled. 'Some great footballers have graced this pitch over the years.'

There was no way of responding to that insult. They simply had to take it on the chin. Sean broke the embarrassed silence after Miller had gone.

'Charming! If that guy's rich enough to own all this, he ought to be able to afford some manners.'

'Our Mr Miller may not be as well off as it appears,' said Ray. 'I've just been speaking to one of their lads' parents. He reckons that Miller's business has gone bust recently. Might even have to sell up.'

Luke gazed around the expanse of land in front of the house, most of which was marked out with soccer pitches. To Luke, it seemed like Paradise. 'Fancy having to leave a place like this. That's terrible.'

'Don't start getting any ideas,' Dad chuckled, seeing the look in his eye. 'You'll be wanting me to buy it off him and move in!'

'I trust you're not still gonna ask Miller for his autograph,' said Titch, Swifts' miniature midfielder.

'Might do,' Luke said with a shrug. 'Anyway, it's up to us to make him eat his words. If we snatch an early goal in the second half, you never know what might happen. Football's a funny old game, as they say.'

'Whoever says that has never played in goal for the Swifts,' muttered Sanjay. 'They'd have lost their sense of humour ages ago.'

'We've got to keep our heads up, men,' Luke told them, ignoring Sanjay's remark. 'Show them we're not gonna go down without a fight.'

'Ever the optimist, our skipper,' said Gregg. 'He'd make the end of the world seem like a good chance to make a fresh start.'

'Well, the end of the world's not the end of the world, is it?'

'Eh?'

'I mean, there's always tomorrow.'

'Tomorrow never comes,' grunted Titch.

'I hope it does this weekend – it's my birthday! And we've got another match tomorrow as well, remember. Jon's playing in that one.'

'Pity he's not playing now,' said Sean. 'Why can't we just bring him on?'

''Cos the skipper's whipped his boots for one thing,' cackled Sanjay.

'Fat lot of good they are without Jon in them. They're just running about all over the place, getting in everybody's way.'

Luke gave Sean a dirty look. 'You know we're only allowed to play Jon on one of the days. That was part of the loan deal with Panthers.'

'Who's gonna tell them? Jon and his dad won't let on.'

'That's not the point. The thing is . . .'

The argument was ended by the referee's whistle and the group broke up before Luke could explain. He was used to that. His team

talks were always being interrupted. He hadn't managed to finish one all season.

There *was* an early goal soon after the restart, but unfortunately not for the Swifts. Sanjay made a complete hash of catching a cross and the number nine tapped the ball over the line for his hat-trick. And then he scored again – and again. Once they had reached double figures, the All Stars turned their team upside down. All the substitutes came on and the keeper swapped places with the five-goal centre-forward. Despite these changes, the score kept mounting, and even the ex-keeper netted twice.

The Swifts left their comeback rather too late. In the dying minutes of the game, Brain at last opened their account with a delicate chip over the sub goalie's head, and then Ricki headed home a corner to make it 13–2. Only the scorer got excited about the goal. Ricki was so carried away, he gathered the ball up and placed it for a conversion attempt.

But there was someone else who would never give up, not until the final whistle, and maybe not even then – the indefatigable skipper. Luke collected a stray ball inside his own penalty area and decided to go on a run. The amused All Stars stood by and let it happen.

*'The skipper's on the ball now, gliding over the halfway line as space appears in front of him. The opposition has backed off, giving him the respect he deserves. Their defence has opened up like the Red Sea . . .'*

Even Luke, at the back of his fertile mind, might have begun to suspect that something wasn't quite right. He'd never been allowed so much time on the ball in his whole career. Somebody normally took it off him within a few seconds, and often it was one of his own teammates.

Time and space seemed to lose reality, as if in a dream. It felt like he was the only player on the pitch. His vision narrowed to the blinkered tunnel ahead of him – and the light at the end of it was the goal itself.

He only tripped over the ball once as he dribbled along, unchallenged, but he still had time to pick himself up and carry on. Suddenly, almost unexpectedly, he found himself in the All Stars goalmouth. He just had the keeper to beat – and even he was leaning on the post. Luke was confused.

'Shoot first, ask questions later,' he decided and then shot.

The ball hit the other post, but luckily bounced

back towards him. He was able to control it, stumble, steady himself again and slice the rebound just wide of the smirking keeper into the net.

'GOOAALL!' he roared and turned, arms aloft, to celebrate.

'Sorry, no goal,' said the referee. 'I'd already blown the whistle.'

'What for? I can't have been offside. I've just run the length of the field.'

'I know. We've all been watching. I blew for the end of the game. They think it's all over – and they're right, it is.'

Luke turned a deep crimson. 'I didn't hear anything,' he said lamely.

The referee smiled. 'Not surprised, lad, the way you were talking to yourself. Still, it's no crime to be so wrapped up in the game.'

Luke trailed away behind his sniggering teammates towards the changing rooms. 'You could have done something to stop me,' he moaned to his dad.

'You were too far gone. Nobody could get a word in edgeways past your commentary. You pretending to be this Bobby Miller or somebody?'

'*Robbie* Miller,' Luke stressed. 'He hated anybody calling him Bobby. Always insisted on

Robbie. It's more Scottish, you see.'

'Well, here he comes now, this *Robbie*, and he still doesn't look too happy. This may not be the best time to ask for his autograph.'

The All Stars coach jabbed a finger at his mobile phone. 'Last time *they* get invited here, I'll see to that,' he was heard to mutter.

He glared at Luke and his dad for a moment before forcing a smile on to his craggy face.

'Look,' began Philip, 'I'm sorry if we . . .'

'Och! Doesna matter now,' said Miller. 'Your Sparrows at least played with a bit o' spirit, kept going right to the end – just like I used to do. Canna stand any team that gives up.'

'Um . . . we're called the *Swifts*, Mr Miller,' Luke said timidly, hoping the great man wouldn't mind being corrected, and then piled on the flattery. 'You were a terrific player, I've read all about you. The way you inspired that famous Scottish win at Wembley, and that brilliant goal you scored in the Cup Final before you got injured . . .'

Luke might have gone on further. He had a knowledge of the game's history as deep as an anorak's pockets, all zipped up so that no tiny detail could ever escape. Miller cut him short.

'Aye, but we still lost – and I never did get a

cup-winners' medal,' he said bitterly and then gave Luke a quizzical look. 'I'm amazed such a wee laddie knows things like that about me nowadays. What's my first name?'

'Robbie, of course,' Luke replied instantly and seized his chance. 'Um . . . please may I have your autograph?'

Miller grinned and pulled out a piece of paper and a pen from his coat pocket to scrawl his name. 'Aye, good job you got that right,' he said, handing over the paper. 'Now, as an extra reward, how would you like to see a lot more old soccer stars tomorrow?'

Luke's excited, flushed face made any words unnecessary and Miller explained his offer. 'I've

organized a wee seven-a-side tournament here in the morning – for charity, y'ken – and I've just had a call from one of the teams. They've cried off and let me down at the last minute. What about you and your Sparrows coming along to make up the numbers, eh?'

Luke overlooked the Sparrows reference this time. 'That'd be brilliant, Mr Miller. You mean, actually play against all the old stars?'

Miller laughed. 'I don't think you're quite up to that, laddie. No, the veterans are putting on an exhibition game to pull in the crowds and raise more money. Their autographs won't come free like mine.'

Philip Crawford tried to curb his son's enthusiasm. 'Well, I'm not sure we could get back tomorrow, Mr Miller. 'You see . . .'

'Plenty of time, Dad,' Luke said quickly. 'We haven't got far to go for the afternoon match, have we? And besides, it *is* my birthday!'

'Right, that's settled,' said Miller. 'Be here ten o'clock sharp for the first match.'

'Can we have our pictures taken with a famous player?' asked Luke, star-struck but not tongue-tied.

Miller's reply, however, left him totally gob-smacked. 'Far better than that, laddie. We've got

something very special coming here tomorrow too. Something even I've never got my hands on before.'

'What's that?' he said breathlessly, hardly daring to guess the answer.

'The F.A. Cup!'

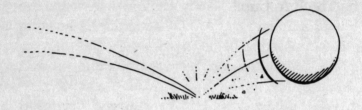

# 5  Bumps in the Night

Room 13 was as dark as a dungeon, but nobody in the six-bed dormitory was asleep. And it wasn't just the sound of Tubs crunching his way through a packet of chocolate biscuits that kept the boys awake.

'It's only a stupid story,' he spluttered, sitting up among the crumbs in his bottom bunk. 'I mean, everybody knows ghosts don't exist.'

'Yeah, right, but even so . . . what if there really was a double murder in this room . . . ?' came a less confident voice from above. Titch hadn't let the heavyweight defender claim the top bunk in case it collapsed and squashed him flat during the night. He'd then needed Tubs's help to clamber up into bed.

His question hung in the air like a bad smell. The possible answer to it was something that had been troubling the footballers ever since the hostel manager had told them the old building was supposed to be haunted.

'Do you reckon the guy was having us on?' asked Gary.

'Well, if he was, it ain't very funny,' muttered his brother below him. 'Why did he have to say it was twin boys that got killed in here?'

'Serves you right,' Brain hissed. 'It was you two who started all this nonsense in the first place, pretending you'd seen a ghost on the stairs. He probably heard you going on about it at tea-time.'

'Look, just shut up, all of you,' demanded Luke. 'Try to get some sleep. We've got a big day ahead of us tomorrow.'

'*Today*, you mean,' Gregg corrected him, peering at the luminous dial of his watch. 'It's just gone midnight.'

Luke's roommates broke into a raucous chorus of '*Happy Birthday, Dear Skipper!*' which helped to take their minds off ghosts, if nothing else.

'Let's celebrate,' cried Tubs. 'I've got a sponge cake in my bag. We can't spend a night in a dorm without having a midnight feast, can we? It's a kind of tradition, like.'

'Just an excuse to feed your fat face again,' laughed Gary as Tubs swung his feet out of bed to fetch the cake.

'Fancy having your thirteenth birthday in room 13,' put in Brain. 'You could even wear the number 13 shirt in the match, Skipper.'

'No, thanks,' snorted Luke. 'I've had enough of Frosty giving me that number for the Comp this season.'

'You've said your precious Johan Cruyff always wore number 14 on his back, even before the days of squad numbers,' Gary reminded him.

'That's different. He was special. He wrote his own rules. He was allowed to wear what he liked.'

Their banter was suddenly interrupted by a loud drumming on the door and the room went very quiet. Tubs even stopped cutting up the cake he was about to share out. Luke waited for Dad's voice telling them to keep the noise down, but the warning failed to come.

'W . . . who is it?' he stuttered. 'W . . . what do you want?'

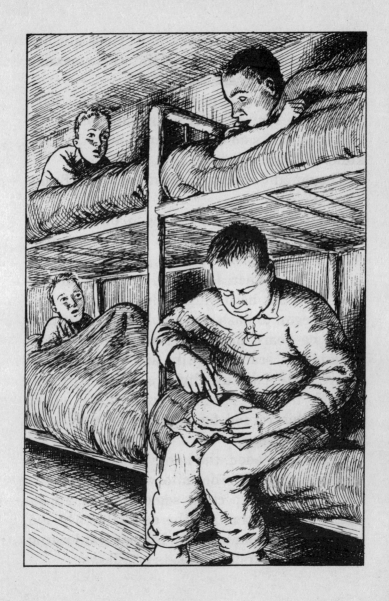

There was no response and Tubs lost his patience. 'Bet it's just some of the others messing about, trying to scare us.'

'They're doing a good job of it too,' Gary whispered. 'I'm not going near that door.'

'Well I am,' said Tubs, brandishing the cake knife. 'If I catch whoever it is, I'll kill 'em.'

'They might already be dead,' snuffled Brain. 'Careful, Tubs.'

'It's a very brave ghost who dares to get between Tubs's belly and his food,' said Gregg. 'That's asking for it.'

Tubs flapped across the cold dormitory floor in bare feet, but he never reached the door. The lights began to flash on and off and eerie music could be heard in the corridor. Tubs scuttled back to bed, scattering cake and biscuits everywhere. His panicky flight seemed strangely slowed in the stroboscopic lighting effect, making his rotund figure look like a gyrating hippo in a disco.

The music faded, the lights went out and the rapping ceased. The dormitory held its collective breath, as if expecting something to appear round or even through the door. But if it did, none of its occupants saw it. Nobody was looking, heads hidden under blankets or pillows.

56

Many minutes passed before Gary nervously risked a peep. 'Er . . . I think it's gone – whatever it was.'

'Go and take a look,' urged his twin.

'You must be joking . . .' he began and then realized that Gregg was next to him in the same bunk. 'Get back down to your own bed, you nutter. What yer doing up here?'

'Dunno, guess it just seemed safer higher up.'

Very little sleep was snatched that night. Even Tubs had lost his appetite, nibbling on a few salvaged biscuits merely for comfort. Only as the first rays of dawn filtered through the curtains did the room feel more normal and the boys manage to doze off.

Not Luke. He was lying on his bunk and gazing at a sheet of paper he had pulled from under his pillow where he'd put it for safe keeping. In the dim light, he could just make out Robbie Miller's autograph.

'Think I'll buy an autograph book with some of my birthday money,' he decided. 'I can make a great start to my collection with Miller and those other old soccer stars too. Maybe I'll even get Johan's one day . . .'

Dreamily, he turned the paper over and saw that there was a sketch map and some writing

on the back. 'Wonder what all this is about?' he mused, sliding his hand under the pillow again to fumble for his little torch. 'Might be important . . .'

It was. But it took Luke's sleep-starved mind several minutes of study in the torchlight to work out just how important. He could barely read the scribbled notes, making out a mention of the F.A. Cup and a million pounds. It was the word *pirates* that puzzled him.

As the shocking truth hit home, a chill ran down his spine. He sat bolt upright. All thoughts of his birthday and even the tour fled in panic. His hands were shaking.

'I don't believe it!' he gasped aloud. 'No, surely not . . .'

At that precise moment, the door burst open. Before Luke could react, he was hauled bodily off his bunk and bundled out of the room. The intruders were no terrifying phantoms. Just a pyjama-clad group of laughing players from another dormitory.

His torch had clattered to the floor, but Luke still clung on to the sheet of paper. He shrieked his protests, waking everyone else up, as they half-dragged, half-carried him along the corridor towards the washroom.

'Let's give him the birthday bumps first,' Sanjay cried over the noise of a gushing shower.

There was nothing Luke could do to stop them. Gripped by half-a-dozen teammates, he was subjected to a limb-wrenching, stomach-churning series of uncoordinated lifts and falls. The count seemed to go on for ever.

'. . . ten . . . eleven . . . twelve . . . and . . . thirteen!' they chanted, almost dropping him by the end through exhaustion.

If Luke thought the ordeal was over, he was wrong.

'Right, now dunk him in here quick,' gasped Big Ben, pulling wide the shower curtain.

The skipper was manhandled across the tiles and forced under the icy cold jets of water. At least he had the satisfaction of making sure that his kidnappers got soaking wet too as they struggled to keep him in place.

'Happy birthday, Skipper!' they cackled before finally letting him escape from his freezing water torture and tossing him a towel.

'Best way to start a day,' sniggered Sanjay, drying his own hair. 'A cold shower really wakes you up.'

'I already *was* awake,' Luke complained, shivering, pulling off the saturated top that clung to him like a second skin. 'Bet it was thanks to you lot I never even got any sleep at all.'

'No idea what you're talking about,' said Big Ben.

'Don't act so innocent. You know what I mean. Acting stupid with the light and music and everything at midnight.'

'Fast asleep we were then, Skip,' said Dazza. 'Never heard a thing.'

Luke suddenly lost interest in their denials. He bent down and picked up a soggy mess from the bottom of the shower cubicle.

'Oh, no!' he groaned. 'Look at this. You've ruined it.'

'Sorry, Skip. What was it? Anything special?'

Luke was devastated. The paper tore into shreds as he tried to open it up. He hadn't just lost Miller's autograph. He'd lost all proof of the Scottish star's outrageous plans to steal the F.A. Cup!

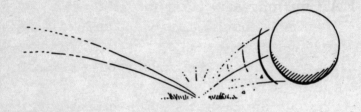

# 6 Birthday Boy

'April Fool!'

'Grow up, will yer!' protested Tubs, finding out too late that there was a layer of salt in the sugar bowl.

Gary laughed. 'You don't mind having a bit of salt on your cornflakes, do you?'

'Yes, I do. April Fool pranks are for little kids.'

'You mean like my kid brother,' he smirked, enjoying the superiority of an extra ten minutes' breathing time over his twin. Gregg had caught him out before breakfast by tying the legs of Gary's jeans into a knot.

The smirk suddenly disappeared. Over the hubbub of voices in the hostel's dining room, Gary had become aware of the sound of music. He grabbed Tubs's arm, making him spill his tea onto the table cloth.

'I'm warning you – cut it out . . .'

Then Tubs heard the music too and stood up, searching for the source.

'Sit down,' Titch complained. 'You're blocking out the light.'

'Shut up and listen. That's what we heard when the ghosts . . .'

Ray Crawford strutted into the room carrying a cassette player. 'Like my soothing music, boys?' he asked with a huge grin.

'Was that you?' demanded his nephew. 'All that banging and stuff?'

'April Fool!' he cried. 'Hope it didn't scare you too much.'

'No, course not,' Gary lied. 'We knew it was somebody playing a joke on us. Gave us a good laugh too, didn't it, Skipper?'

Luke's muttered agreement did not sound very convincing and his dad handed him a parcel. 'Happy birthday, Luke – your first day as a teenager. I trust this will make up for any lost beauty sleep last night.'

Luke tore open the wrapping paper and held up an orange football shirt for all to see. He had a Holland kit at home, but the style was out of date and the number nine shirt was now a bit small for him. This one was emblazoned with the name CRUYFF above his hero's legendary number 14. The room dissolved into laughter.

Luke's pleasure at the gift was diluted by the dark cloud that hung over him. He'd hardly tasted his breakfast, too busy brooding about the threat to the F.A. Cup. He still hadn't told anybody what he thought Miller was up to. The

incriminating evidence had been washed away.

'Thanks, Dad,' he managed to say. 'Just what I wanted. Pity I'm not fourteen today, I guess.'

'Superstar!' cried Sanjay. 'With that shirt and Jon's boots, there'll be no stopping our skipper now.'

'Yeah, but Jon needs his boots back today,' Sean pointed out.

'Hope so. What's the squad for the Sevens, Skipper?' the goalkeeper asked. 'Have you sorted it out yet?'

Luke sighed. He'd almost forgotten about the tournament. Deciding on which players and tactics to employ had helped him to while away the sleepless hours, but it now all seemed so trivial.

'Well, there's me of course,' he began, 'then cousins Jon and Ricki . . .'

'This is starting to sound like a family show,' Tubs guffawed. 'You'll be telling us next that your dad and uncle are turning out too!'

'Does that mean I can't play this afternoon now?' Jon piped up.

'No problem, the way I see it,' Luke explained. 'The Panthers only banned you from playing both days. They said nothing about you not playing twice on the same day.'

'Nice one, Boss,' Jon smiled.

'Anyway, I've picked an eight-man squad, so the rest are Sanjay, Brain, Big Ben, Gary and Titch. We'll use a basic 2–2–2 formation, OK?'

Nobody could be bothered to argue. They rarely kept to their positions during a game in any case. Even Sanjay had been known to wander upfield at times for a strike at the other goal.

As the boys left the dining room, Gary went up to Ray. 'Er . . . there is just one thing I've been wondering about. How did you do the trick with the flashing lights?'

'Never touched the light switch,' he replied, puzzled. 'You must have been imagining that . . .'

*

The Swifts arrived at Tibworth Manor to find the playing area already swarming with people. Some of those wearing soccer boots were also in fancy dress. They were college students out to have fun and raise money for charity at the same time. All the teams in the different age-group competitions were being sponsored for every goal scored.

There were teams of cowboys and indians, pantomime dames, spacemen, animals and teddy bears, and even a side made up of seven

Elvis Presleys. But the group of players that immediately caught Luke's eye was the one in pirate outfits.

'Glad you made it on time, Sparrows,' Robbie Miller welcomed them as they reported in. 'Your first match is on that far pitch.'

'Nobody told us we were supposed to be sponsored,' said Ray.

'I'll sponsor you myself. What shall we say – a hundred pounds a goal?' he chuckled and the boys gasped. 'From what I saw of you Sparrows yesterday, I don't reckon it's gonna cost me very much.'

A helicopter appeared out of the clouds and Miller squinted up towards it. 'Aye, good, right on cue. You can all do your bit by paying to pose with this.'

'What, the chopper?' said Sanjay.

'Nay, what's inside it, laddie. Had it flown in, special delivery.'

The helicopter circled the grounds twice and came down to settle on a landing pad next to the manor. Before the blades had even stopped whirling, a security guard stepped out with a gleaming trophy cradled in his burly arms.

'Wow! Just look at that,' cried Brain in excitement. 'The F.A. Cup!'

'What a treat for the birthday boy!' grinned Sanjay. 'We'll never hear the last of this.'

The Cup was placed on a display table near the pitches and a queue immediately began to form for the official photographer.

'It's up to me,' Luke said to himself, gazing in awe at the world-famous trophy. 'I've just got to do something to stop it being pinched.'

Luke's dad had washed the Swifts' all-gold kit in the hostel laundry room and issued a warning as he dished it out to the players. 'Don't get this dirty, lads. You've got to wear it again this afternoon.'

Luke was changing in silence in a corner of the dressing room when he suddenly realized that his teammates were all staring at him.

'Um . . . what do you want?' he said, as if coming out of a trance.

'We're waiting for you to do your little party piece,' said Sanjay.

'Oh, leave it, not important, off you go. I'll join you in a minute.'

The Swifts looked at each other in astonishment. They had never seen Luke so downbeat before a game of football.

'Cheer up, Skipper, it's your birthday,' said Gary.

'What's this party piece?' asked Jon.

'He goes, "Right, men. All ready?" and we go, "Ready, Skipper!" ' Brain explained. 'We always do it before a match.'

'Doesn't matter if we give it a miss for once, does it?' snapped Luke. 'Look, I've just got things on my mind, OK? I'm not in the mood.'

The others trooped outside, leaving only Jon behind with Luke. 'C'mon, out with it. What's up? You can tell me.'

'I've got to tell somebody or I'll burst. Something terrible's going to happen this morning.' Luke glanced around to ensure they were completely alone and then sat his cousin down. 'Promise you won't let on to anybody?'

Jon nodded. 'Course. Anything you say.'

As Luke unburdened himself about what he'd discovered on the back of his autographed paper, Jon's eyes grew wider and wider.

'You positive, Luke?' he exclaimed. 'You're saying Miller's plotting to nick the F.A. Cup and ransom it for a million quid?'

'You see, even you don't believe me. That's why I haven't told our dads – or even the police. Miller would only deny it and then I'd be the one in trouble for wasting police time.'

Jon gave his habitual little shrug. 'At least

you'd ruin his plans. Miller wouldn't dare do anything after you'd reported it.'

'Yeah, suppose so,' Luke sighed. 'But I don't want to risk it, just in case I *am* wrong. I could never live that down. He was a great player once, you know.'

'Seems like he's just a crook now. He must be really desperate for money to try and pull a stunt like this in front of all these people.'

'I think there might be more to it than that.'

'How d'yer mean?'

'Remember I said he broke his leg in the Cup Final? Well, that injury more or less finished his career. He was never the same player after-wards from what I've read.'

'So?'

'So maybe he's got some kind of grudge against the Cup and this is his strange way of getting his own back on it.'

Jon shrugged again. 'Possible, I guess. Anyway, what are we gonna do about it? You've had more time to think about this than me.'

'Knew I could count on you, Johan,' said Luke in relief. 'Best thing to do, I reckon, is let the snatch actually take place first – but Robbie Miller's not the only one who's got a plan. Listen . . .'

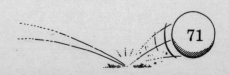

# 7   At Sixes & Sevens

'Oh, well,' sighed Titch. 'At least we earned a hundred quid.'

The Sparrows – as they were known in the tournament – were on the wrong end of a 5–1 scoreline in the opening game of their three-team group.

'Makes a nice change to get paid for being thrashed,' said Big Ben. 'We usually do it for nothing.'

They had found themselves up against Hart-bridge Harriers, the same opponents they were due to meet that afternoon. The Harriers had practised hard for this tournament and it showed. Their slick teamwork was in stark contrast to Luke's makeshift squad, slung together over breakfast, who performed like a bunch of strangers.

Luke himself was virtually a non-playing captain, unable to raise any enthusiasm for the contest. Even his inbuilt commentator was off-duty and the action passed him by in an uncanny silence. Luke's lack of involvement might well have been to their advantage in the Sunday League, but carrying a passenger in a seven-a-side match proved too much of a handicap.

Jon appeared equally distracted, although he did manage to put the ball in the net for a profit-able consolation goal. Only the fact that the game was a mere seven minutes each-way saved them from a worse drubbing.

'Waste of time Luke wearing my boots,' grum-bled Gregg. 'He could've just wandered about in his slippers.'

They had a while to wait before what was certain to be their second and last game of the tournament. The whole touring party made their way towards the busy photographer, with Luke and Jon trailing along behind.

'What time did you say was on that bit of paper?' asked Jon.

'11.30 – that's during the veterans' challenge match. Clever, eh? Gives Miller a perfect alibi for when the Cup actually gets whipped.'

'By the Pirates?'

'Looks like it,' said Luke, gazing towards a pitch where the students were playing. Someone with a plastic parrot on his shoulder had just blasted the ball over the bar. 'It's not the original F.A. Cup, you know. That vanished from a shop window display. They reckon it was melted down into silver coins.'

Jon was shocked. 'When did that happen?'

'Oh, over a hundred years ago – 1896.'

'Wondered why I hadn't heard about it on the

news,' he sighed. He might have guessed that Luke would know some useless fact like that.

When their turn finally came in front of the camera, the cousins held up the F.A. Cup between them. It was a bittersweet moment. Under normal circumstances, it would have been the soccer highlight of their lives. But it was ruined by the knowledge that, if things went wrong, *they* could be the ones to blame this time for the loss of such a priceless trophy.

Luke astonished his teammates by announcing that he was not playing in the next match. He used the excuse that he wanted to give Titch a full game.

'Must be ill,' muttered Big Ben, tugging on the captain's armband.

'Think I know the real reason,' grinned Tubs, spotting the roaming packs of autograph-hunters. 'If there's one thing that might stop Luke from playing, it's a chance like this to mingle with all them old stars he's always banging on about.'

Tubs wasn't too far wrong, but Luke also needed to be free to keep an eye on Miller and the Pirates. He only watched the first few minutes of their game against the Red Dragons

before slipping away. His absence wasn't noticed until there was nobody to give the half-time team talk, and by then they were 2–0 down.

'Told you,' Tubs said triumphantly. 'Luke's over there, look, trying to get some bloke's autograph. He doesn't care what's happening to us.'

'Who is it?' asked Brain.

'Dunno. He's so old, he must have died before we were born!'

Luke was in his element, surrounded by so many ex-internationals. He recognized most of them, despite their disguises of paunches, glasses and bald heads. He'd already collected five autographs in the back of his notebook when he saw Miller talking to the Pirates.

'The double-crosser!' Luke cursed. 'Bet they've got no idea what he's really up to. They probably think it's just a publicity stunt for charity or something. Huh! The only cause he's interested in helping is his own.'

Meanwhile, Luke's neglected 'Swallows' were staging a comeback. Jon weaved in and out of a couple of tackles and set up his Italian cousin for a pop at goal. Ricki almost put it over the crossbar, rugby-style, but the ball dipped at the last moment, clipped the underside of the wood-work and buried itself in the netting.

'Great goal, Ricki!' cried Big Ben. 'That's a plenty big hole in Miller's wallet. Let's have another now.'

They certainly had their opponents worried. Titch's fierce tackling in midfield had snuffed out the flames of the Dragons' attacks and Gary found space to move forward and support Brain up the left-flank. For a while the Dragons resisted, but finally caved in and surrendered their lead.

The equalizer was well deserved. Gary and Brain linked up neatly along the touchline until the winger had a clear sight of goal. His aim was lethal. Before any defender could close him down, Brain drove the ball low into the gap

between the keeper and his near post. The ball seemed to pick up speed off the wet grass and left the keeper groping.

'Double your money, Miller!' roared Tubs from the touchline. 'The Sparrows are flying high!'

The game ended as a 2–2 draw, confirming the Harriers as group winners and destined for a clash with Tibworth All Stars in the Final.

'D'yer reckon Luke might stand down again this afternoon?' said Titch. 'We might give the Harriers more of a fight of it then.'

'No chance!' laughed Tubs. 'You'll have to put up with both him and me again in the full team.'

Jon left the others to celebrate their mini-success. He pulled on his tracksuit top and went to find Luke at their pre-arranged meeting place in the car park. 'Drew, two each,' he reported. 'Did OK without you.'

'What do you mean by that?' Luke snorted.

Jon tried to rephrase his remark more kindly. 'I mean, your team did well to overcome the loss of their skipper,' he smiled. 'Your fighting spirit must have rubbed off on them. They did you proud.'

'Should think so too after all my coaching. Miller's gonna regret the day he tangled with the Sparrows, er . . . I mean the Swifts.'

'Did you find out anything more?'

'Well, I saw the Pirates moving their minibus into a different position facing the trophy table. I think I know what's likely to happen now. I'll tell you on the way to the summerhouse. We'd better go and get in position before things hot up round here.'

Using the cluster of vehicles in the car park to shield their furtive exit, the cousins disappeared round the side of Tibworth Manor. The rear gardens were more extensive than they had imagined.

'So where's this summerhouse of his?' said Jon as they trotted through the trees.

'How should I know? His diagram wasn't to scale, you know. He'd just drawn some arrows pointing to it on the map, so I'm assuming that's where they're going to stash the Cup. Can't be too far away.'

They found the small stone building nestling in bushes close to a country lane that ran along the length of the estate. Luke was all for going up immediately to check what was inside, but Jon held him back.

'Let's wait here under cover for a bit, OK? Y'know, stake the place out like they do in films – just in case.'

'In case of what?'

'Dunno. Just in case . . .' said Jon. 'Miller must realize the grounds will be searched by the police. He could have his own men lurking about, ready to take the Cup somewhere safer after it's been dumped here.'

'Hmm, good thinking, Johan,' Luke admitted, wishing he'd thought of that himself. They might have walked straight into an ambush.

The exhibition game, England versus Scotland, was now entertaining the spectators before the various Finals took place. The veterans had lost few of their ball skills and the generous applause carried to the boys as they crouched behind some shrubs thirty metres from the summerhouse.

'Sorry to be missing that,' murmured Luke, his breathing rapid and shallow. 'I'd have loved to see all those great players in action . . .'

He paused. Angry cries drifted across the gardens, much different to the previous crowd noises.

'Guess the Pirates have struck,' said Jon. 'If you're right, they should show up here in a couple of minutes.'

'This is it!' hissed Luke, unable to contain his excitement. He was trembling from head to

studded boots. 'Get ready to repel boarders!'

The pirate raid had lasted no more than twenty seconds. As the minibus skidded to a halt beside the table, two of the students jumped out, snatched the trophy and dived back in. By the time either the photographer or security guard could react, the driver was already revving away. He ploughed across one of the pitches, gouging deep tyre tracks in the soft earth as he headed for the front gates.

Few of the spectators enjoying the football were even aware of the drama at first. Nor were the players – except for one. Robbie Miller watched the minibus roar off down the road, and then had to wipe the grin from his face as one of

the tournament organizers raced towards him.

'Sorry, guys, got to go,' he excused himself, calling for a substitute to take his place. 'Something must have cropped up.'

'They've stolen the F.A. Cup!' the official wailed.

'What! Who have?' growled Miller.

'Pirates, Mr Miller – I mean, some of the students . . .'

'Stop babbling, man. What did they look like?'

'Er . . . one had a patch over his eye, and the other was wearing a three-cornered hat with a parrot on his shoulder . . .'

His voice trailed away as he realized how ridiculous that sounded.

'Och! The police are gonna love those descriptions,' Miller said sarcastically, as if genuinely angry. 'Can't wait till I see the thieves' photo-fit pictures on TV!'

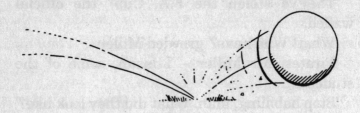

# 8   April Fool

The minibus pulled up on the country lane next to a padlocked gate. Luke and Jon ducked further down in the shrubbery, but the students were in too much of a hurry to check whether anybody else was about.

A couple of them climbed over the gate with the Cup, ran towards the summerhouse and disappeared inside. Seconds later, they were sprinting for the bus, empty-handed, and it accelerated away in a cloud of exhaust fumes.

'Right, time for us to move quick too,' said Luke. 'Let's go and grab the Cup before any real baddies get here.'

'What if they're already here, watching and waiting like us?'

'All the more reason for acting now,' Luke urged. 'C'mon, we'll just have to chance our luck.'

They left their shelter and broke into a crab-like jog across the open space to the summerhouse. Only upon reaching its stone wall did they remember to breathe again.

'Hear anything?' gasped Jon.

'Only my heart thumping. Or is that yours?'

'Best if one of us stays outside to keep a look-out. You or me?'

'You,' said Luke. 'I'm going in. Keep me covered, OK?'

'What with? Just go and get it, will you, and then we can leg it fast. I'll whistle if I see anybody.'

Luke barged through the door and immediately stumbled over a broken chair. 'I'm OK,' he called out. 'It's just a bit dark in here.'

The building clearly wasn't in use much, apart from as a store for old garden furniture and machinery – and now the F.A. Cup. It stood on the floor in the far corner behind a rusted lawn-mower.

Luke would never view the trophy the same way again. It was like finding a beautiful

princess sleeping in the slums. Whenever some victorious team captain proudly held the F.A. Cup up high in front of the royal box at Wembley Stadium, he would picture it among the dirt and debris of this dingy room.

'C'mon, hurry up,' Jon hissed. 'Are you posing with it in there?'

It broke the spell and Luke's fanciful mind clicked back into gear. He lifted the Cup carefully, making sure he didn't scratch it against the mower, and then made for the door.

Jon tried to whistle, but his mouth had suddenly gone dry. 'Wait . . .' he croaked but it was too late. Luke was already stepping outside.

Two men were clambering over the gate from the lane. As they landed on the grass and turned, they saw the boys too. Or at least the back of them. The cousins were in full flight through the tangle of bushes, fleeing in the general direction of the manor. Luke had pushed the heavy, circular base into Jon's midriff and was carrying the rest himself, Cup under one arm and its lid in his other hand.

'Hey! Come back!' came a yell, but they were in no mind to obey.

Then came another command. 'Stop or I'll shoot!'

That one made them think for a moment – but not stop and think. They charged on, heaving for breath in their panic, expecting any moment the sound of gunfire and a whistling bullet. They wouldn't have had time to read whose name might have been on it.

They heard nothing but a lot of swearing. If Tubs had been with them, they might have had a problem, but both Luke and Jon were fitter than their pursuers. And the fear of being caught spurred them on to set Olympic qualifying times for any sprint event that involved carrying silverware.

They didn't stop running until they reached the manor house itself. The boys leant against its red-brick walls to try and recover their breath and their shattered nerves. There was no sign of anyone behind them.

'Reckon . . . they were . . . bluffing . . . 'bout the gun . . . ?' gasped Jon.

'Dunno . . . but . . . think we've . . . lost 'em . . .' gulped Luke, sliding down the wall to sit on the gravel. 'We won . . . Johan . . . we won the Cup!'

It was painful to laugh. Their lungs didn't yet have enough air in them. As their pulse rates gradually subsided, Jon posed another question

that was beginning to bother him. 'So . . . what do we do with it now?'

Luke looked up and blinked. He hadn't thought his own plan through as far as that. 'Put it back on the table?' he said lamely.

'Oh yeah? We casually stroll up and say, "Oh, look what we've just found!" Come off it.'

'Hmm, I see what you mean. Tricky, this.'

'Could be your chance to play the big hero. You'd be on the telly and all the front pages – *The Birthday Boy who saved the F.A. Cup.*'

'Not just me. Both of us,' said Luke, conjuring up even more dramatic headlines. 'It'd be like Pickles all over again.'

'Pickles?'

'Yeah, you know, the dog which went out for a walk one day in 1966 and found the missing World Cup. He became famous.'

'Is that what you want? Fame?'

Luke was sorely tempted, but then gave a heavy sigh and scrambled to his feet. 'No, not really – well, not yet, anyway. Too much explaining to do. I just want to go and play football this afternoon.'

'Good,' said his cousin with relief. 'C'mon, let's just dump the Cup where somebody will soon find it.'

'Another Pickles-wannabe, perhaps. That'd make a good story.'

They crept back into the car park, twice having to dodge down out of sight behind vehicles as somebody approached.

'We can just stick it up on one of the car bonnets and melt away into the crowd,' said Jon.

'OK, but hold on. Wait a minute. I've had an idea.'

Jon groaned. 'You and your ideas. Look, if you ever decide to go on another tour, just leave me out of it, right. I prefer a quiet life.'

Luke had ripped a page out of his notebook and rested it on the ground while he scribbled something. 'Ready now. Let's do it.'

The base and the trophy, complete with lid, suddenly appeared on a bonnet, with a torn piece of paper trapped underneath. The message read:

The F.A. Cup was soon whirling away into the sky to return to the dull safety of the club's trophy cabinet. Its adventures were over.

The tournament was over too. The Finals had been duly completed and Robbie Miller had the small consolation that his All Stars team had defeated the Harriers 3–1. He had not, otherwise, had a good day. Even his beloved Scotland had lost 4–2.

He didn't understand at first how the plan could have failed and how the Cup had turned up again in the car park. Then his men told him of the two boys at the summerhouse. His heart sank. A frantic search of his pockets confirmed his worst fears. The paper with all his notes on was missing.

'That autograph yesterday,' he remembered. 'That idiot Sparrows captain who knew all about me – and who now knows even more!'

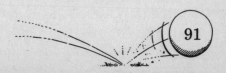

Miller found Luke eating a picnic lunch on a grassy bank with his teammates and indicated that he'd like a private word.

'Now then, laddie, have you still got that piece of paper I gave you?'

Luke knew that feigning ignorance would be a waste of time. 'You mean the one with your autograph on it? And something on the back . . . ?'

The subject of their conversation did not need to be mentioned. Miller forced a crooked smile, struggling to control his temper. He knew full well that this boy could make things very nasty for him. 'Aye, that's the one. I trust nobody else has seen it? Like your pal, for instance . . .'

Luke shook his head and Miller eyed him suspiciously, uncertain whether to believe him. 'Aye, good. Well, I'd like it back – please. I'm willing to pay you quite a lot of money for it.'

'I don't want your money, Mr Miller,' Luke replied seriously. 'But I'm sure an extra donation to the students' charities would be appreciated. That might help to keep the Pirates quiet if the police question them.'

Miller nodded. He knew when he was beaten, even though Luke finally confessed that the vital evidence had been destroyed. Just to be on the safe side, Miller produced something from

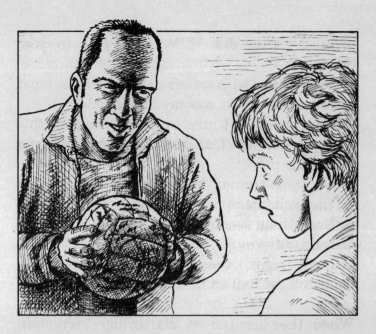

his sports bag that he hoped would ensure Luke's silence too. It was the football used in the exhibition match, signed by all the stars, including Miller himself.

'Our wee secret, eh, laddie?' he said, handing over the souvenir ball.

It was an offer that Luke could not refuse. He sat nursing the football next to Brain on the minibus for the short drive to Hartbridge. The winger was admiring all the autographs, despite the fact that he couldn't read any of them.

'Their writing's worse than mine,' Brain

grinned. 'Why did Miller give this to you, Skipper?'

Luke smiled with satisfaction. 'Guess he must have known that it was my birthday.'

'Hope you didn't miss all the excitement this morning with the Cup and that. Where did you disappear to?'

'Oh, I was around,' he said casually. 'And I had all the excitement I needed, thanks, don't worry.'

'Everything seems to have worked out OK in the end, anyway.'

'Dead right, there, Brain,' he chuckled, bouncing the ball on his lap.

When they arrived at Hartbridge recreation ground, the Harriers captain came up to challenge them. 'What are you lot doing here? We're playing the Swifts this afternoon.'

'That's us – and we're here for revenge!' Luke replied. 'Swifts are much quicker and more skilful than sparrows.'

The Swifts soon discovered that their skipper was back to his usual bubbly self. Luke flitted about the changing room, reminding everybody of their positions in the 4–3–3 formation he had devised to accommodate Jon. Gregg was not best pleased to be among the subs.

'Just a temporary sacrifice for the good of the team, Gregg, OK?' Luke wheedled. 'You'll be on at half-time, promise.'

The player-manager had to work hard to convince their regular striker that it wasn't just because he needed to borrow his boots again.

'Right, men,' cried Luke to gain everyone's attention. 'All ready?'

'Ready, Skipper,' they responded loudly.

'Welcome back, Skip,' laughed Dazza. 'You sound on form again.'

'I just don't know how we managed without you earlier,' said Sanjay, doing well to keep a straight face. 'Got it all sorted, did you, whatever was bothering you?'

Luke glanced at Jon who gave him a little warning shake of the head. They'd agreed not to tell *anybody* about their dramatic rescue act.

'Yeah, no problems. Now today's my birthday and I want . . .'

He was interrupted again, this time by Tubs. 'Is it, Skipper? Oh, you should have said. We'd have got you something.'

Everyone burst out laughing. Luke had only mentioned his birthday about a thousand times since the tour was first arranged.

'Anyway,' he continued, 'I want us to celebrate

with a win and end the tour on a high note . . .'

Sean let out a piercing shriek, making them all cover their ears.

'What the hell was that for?' gasped Sanjay.

'That's about as high a note as I can reach,' he grinned.

'About time your voice broke, then,' Mark muttered, as deeply as he could manage.

Luke gave up. 'OK, men, let's just get out there and show these Harriers how the Swifts can really play.'

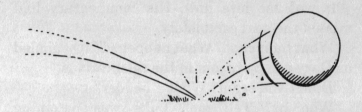

# 9 Un-Friendly

Luke was determined to enjoy himself in this match now that he could concentrate purely on football again. Although it was a strain to keep the secret bottled up, his commentary at least gave him a broadcasting outlet as a safety valve. After all, nobody was listening.

*'The unsung hero of the morning, Luke Crawford, kicks off the final game of the Swifts' eventful Easter tour and the ball goes out to Dazza on the right-wing. It has been an amazing birthday for the skipper. If it weren't for him, the F.A. Cup would . . .'*

He broke off. He suddenly realized that the ball was in the back of the Harriers' net. Luke had been so concerned with setting the scene and getting in an early mention of the Cup that he hadn't even started to describe the action.

It was too late now. His commentary had missed the goal completely.

'What happened? What happened?' he gabbled as Gary ran by to join in the celebrations.

'Didn't you see it? What a header!'

'Who by? Tell me!' Luke was becoming desperate, but Gary was gone.

Luke followed and threw himself onto the top of the mêlée of gold shirts. Only as the bodies began to part did he discover that cousin Ricki was at the bottom of the pile.

'Brill, Ricki!' cried Luke. 'How did you do it?'

Ricki looked dazed, partly through oxygen starvation underneath the crush. 'Eh? Not me. I no score.'

'Well, who did then?'

'Their number five. Plenty great own goal!'

The Harriers' central defender was still sitting on the grass in disbelief. He had risen to meet the winger's cross and hadn't expected the aerial challenge that put him off. The ball glanced off the side of his head into the far corner of the net,

leaving the goalkeeper speechless – if only for a few seconds. His teammate was making up for it now, standing over him and still finding new, colourful ways of abusing the big defender.

Ricki deserved the credit for his part in the shock goal. Only someone with his level of fitness would have reached the goalmouth in time to leap high for Dazza's overhit centre and force the error.

The blue-shirted Harriers were quick to vent their anger at conceding such a goal. The captain's father had volunteered to referee this

so-called friendly game and he turned an indulgent blind eye to the many fouls committed, especially by his son.

*'Looks like the Swifts are up against twelve men here,'* muttered the commentary. *'The player-manager will have to make sure that his own team don't retaliate or things could turn ugly. The Swifts must keep trying to play good clean football . . .'*

Luke hopelessly mistimed his next tackle. He stuck out a leg as an opponent dribbled past him, missed the ball, but not the player. The attacker crumpled to the ground as if shot by a sniper – and the ground happened to be inside the penalty area.

'Accidental, ref, honest!' Luke claimed as the man pointed to the spot. 'I went for the ball.'

'No arguing, lad. You're lucky not to get sent off.'

The penalty-taker sent Sanjay the wrong way to level the scores and the rot set in. By half-time the Swifts were in an all-too-familiar position.

'Oh, well, only losing 3–1,' said Mark. 'Could be worse.'

'It usually is,' sighed Big Ben. 'Skipper's only managed to trip one of them up in the area so far.'

Luke pulled a face. 'Can't help it. I don't do it on purpose.'

'Could have fooled me,' grunted Tubs. 'Just how many pens have you given away this season, Skipper?'

'Bet that's one statistic he doesn't keep in his little black book!' Sanjay scoffed. 'Boy, would I love to get a read of that! It must be hilarious.'

Luke had deliberately not brought his official record book on tour. He was frightened of it falling into the wrong hands – Sanjay's, for instance. He knew it was one thing that the goalkeeper wouldn't let slip through his fingers. Not like the third goal.

'They're just a bunch of dirty foulers,' complained Titch. 'Should've had a penalty ourselves when Brain got kicked up in the air.'

'It shows we've earned their respect,' Luke said in encouragement. 'Teams only bother kicking opponents they think can outplay them.'

'Reckon I'd rather not be kicked,' said Dazza. 'Respect is too hard on the shins.'

'Well, you can rub them better this half,' replied Luke. 'Gregg's playing on the wing now, OK? He can't wait to get kicked about.'

There was a lot of fuss as Gregg demanded his boots back. Dazza's were much too big for Luke,

but Sean was coming off too and was reluctantly persuaded to part with his.

'Only if you clean them up during the holidays,' he insisted. 'And make sure you do a good job of it too, Skipper.'

Luke himself had been a target for Harriers' cloggers, mainly because they were fed up of having his commentary buzzing in their ears like an irritating insect that won't go away. Luke borrowed Sean's shinpads too and fastened them inside his socks as a double layer of protection.

The second half began in similar vein. Luke was painfully floored in the centre-circle by a sly kick, but it was difficult to keep him quiet. He bounced back up, as always, and resumed his commentary just as Brain and the ball had been deposited unceremoniously over the touchline together. All they got was a throw-in.

*'Disgraceful decision by the referee! Undeterred, Ricki throws the ball in to Brain who bravely takes on the defender again and this time slips the ball through his legs. A perfect nutmeg. That's the way to hit back. Johan's on the ball now just outside the area. He's been having a bit of a quiet game so far, but this looks dangerous – ohhh! Referee!'*

Jon had been crudely scythed down by the number five and at last the referee could find no excuse not to give a free-kick. Luke positioned the ball just inside the 'D', a little to the left of centre of the goal, as the Harriers formed a defensive wall.

'That's nowhere near ten yards,' Luke claimed. 'Move them back, ref.'

The appeal was ignored.

'Deaf as well as blind,' muttered Brain, the Swifts' dead-ball specialist, but Jon wanted to take this kick himself.

Luke saw the glint in his cousin's eye and knew he meant business. The foul had riled him.

*'The Harriers may live to regret what they've just done,'* murmured the commentary, *sotto voce* for a change, so as not to forewarn the opposition. *'They've woken up Jon Crawford, the Swifts' multi-talented guest star.'*

'Doesn't matter about the wall, Luke,' Jon told him. 'The ball's going over it into the top corner.'

It did, too. Jon curled the ball with the inside of his right foot up and over the barricade before it dipped late and thwacked into the netting beyond the keeper's dive. It was a touch of real class.

Jon ran the show for the next ten minutes and treated the spectators, including the unemployed Sanjay, to the whole range of his wonderful skills. His equalizer came from a sweetly struck left-foot volley as cousin Ricki's chipped pass reached him just inside the area. The goalkeeper didn't even bother to move for this screamer.

'Stop this guy!' cried the captain. 'Kill him before he murders us.'

They couldn't stop him, not now Jon was in this mood. Even his dad had never seen him so hot. He was much too quick for defenders who tried to chop him down, riding their clumsy tackles with balletic grace and dodging any attempts to trip, push and kick him out of his stride.

The Swifts did not have long to wait for Jon's hat-trick goal. Luke fed him the ball in the centre-circle and then watched Jon take off as if chased by a couple of gunmen again. After fleeing from a bullet, the Harriers defence held no terrors for him.

Luke's commentary might have exaggerated slightly in saying that Jon left six opponents trailing in his wake, but nobody was counting. The poor goalkeeper was resigned to his fate. Jon

took great delight in dribbling round him before scoring, teasing him like a kitten with a ball of wool.

The Harriers were now completely unravelled. Although Jon's appetite for goals was at last satisfied, the home team's morale was in tatters and the inspired Swifts comfortably defended the 4–3 lead he had given them.

Even the allowance of extra added time by the referee failed to produce an equalizer and he eventually had to blow the final whistle. The Swifts had won and Jon was carried from the pitch, shoulder-high, in triumph.

It was a happy, noisy journey home in the crowded minibus. The weekend trip had turned out better than Luke would have dared to predict. He was tucked up by a window, contentedly mulling over what he was going to write for his next report in the *Swillsby Chronicle*, the monthly village newspaper edited by Uncle Ray.

When they stopped at a service station for petrol and refreshments, Luke suddenly found himself the centre of attention. Tubs handed over a brown paper bag.

'Here you are, Skipper,' he grinned. 'Happy birthday from all your teammates. Sorry it's not wrapped or anything.'

Luke opened the bag and pulled out a large, black notebook. He looked up at them in surprise.

'Hope this might make up for your soaking this morning and show we love you really,' laughed Sanjay.

'What's it for?'

'Next season, stupid. So you'll be able to write up all the details of our matches then as well. You must've nearly filled the old one by now.'

'You mean you still want to play for the Swifts next season?'

'Course we do,' said Big Ben. 'Even if we do end up getting relegated. Who else would have us useless lot, eh?'

Luke could not have had a better birthday present. Even the ball and Cruyff's number 14 shirt paled by comparison. Nothing could mean more to him than having the support of his team-mates, even if they did sometimes have a strange way of showing it.

'You're not useless,' he said, fighting back the tears he felt welling up inside. 'Far from it. To me, you're all soccer stars!'

THE END

# CRAWFORD'S CORNER

Hi! Luke Crawford here again. Hope you enjoyed reading about the Swifts' Easter tour and my adventures with the F.A. Cup. You now know that you'll have me to thank if you ever get the chance to hold up that famous trophy on Cup Final day in front of the royal box at Wembley Stadium. Come on, admit it, I bet you've dreamt of that, haven't you? All soccer mad kids do.

Some great players have actually had that proud moment, but not many of the ones featured here in *Crawford's Corner*. Yep, this is the part of the book where they let me write my own piece without the author or anybody getting in the way. I don't even give Uncle Ray the chance to edit it. He'd only want me to change things, like with my match reports for his newspaper, the *Swillsby Chronicle*. This is straight from me to you.

I want to tell you this time about some of the old

soccer stars, just like the ones whose autographs I got in this story. (Not Robbie Miller, though. Best to leave him out of this after what happened!) I think it's important for all young soccer fans to know something about the really great players who have graced the 'beautiful game', as football is often called. I've had to do some research on this subject in all my soccer reference books as I've decided to stick just to men who have now had to hang up their boots. Modern players like Ronaldo, Roberto Carlos, Giggs, Zidane, Del Piero, Bergkamp, Shearer, Maldini, etc., etc., might well be very good – but true *greatness* has to stand the test of time. We'll have to let history be their judge.

It's been dead fascinating to read all about such stars again. Why not get down to your local library and borrow a book or two yourself to find out lots more about these 'golden oldies'?

Let me start you off. Bet you can't guess who I reckon is the greatest footballer of all time! No, not Pelé. I'll come to him later. You know who I mean really – the fantastic, magnificent, supreme **Johan Cruyff** of course, often known as the Flying Dutchman. My mates say I'm always going on

about him – and why not? I could write a whole book about his wonderful talents. In fact, I probably will do one day when I'm a soccer journalist.

Pelé might well be the most *famous* footballer in the world but – in my opinion at least – the *best* has surely got to be my hero, Johan Cruyff. He's even been a top coach after his fabulous playing days were over, winning four Spanish league championships in a row for Barcelona and also the European Cup. (That's the competition we now call the Champions League.) He played for Barcelona, too, after leading Ajax to three successive European Cup triumphs in '71, '72, & '73. He won the '72 Final virtually on his own, destroying Inter Milan with his skills and scoring both goals in their 2–0 victory. No wonder he was voted European Footballer of the Year three times. Johan also skippered Holland brilliantly in the '74 World Cup in West Germany, scoring the decisive second goal in their 2–0 semi-final win over the holders, Brazil. Unluckily, the Dutch lost 2–1 in the Final itself to the Germans.

Johan Cruyff was the complete footballer. He had everything: pace, acceleration, instant ball control, amazing balance and superb passing

skills – and he also scored loads of goals. He was so versatile and original, even inventing a new ingenious piece of dribbling trickery that had never been seen before. Well, he *was* a genius. It's now known as the 'Cruyff Turn'.

I'd better move on to somebody else, I guess, before I get totally carried away. If there was one player who made a shirt number more celebrated than Johan's number 14, it must be the number 10 of Brazil's Edson Arantes do Nascimento. Who? **Pelé**, of course. A bit easier and quicker to scrawl in autograph books, that's for sure. Many Brazilians are better known by their nicknames, although Pelé doesn't know where his came from. He didn't even like it at first, getting into fights at school when other kids teased him with it. In his own family, he's still called by a different pet name altogether, Dico. There you are, another bit of useful soccer trivia for you to come out with one day and impress all your mates.

Pelé had a phenomenal goalscoring record, notching up 1,283 goals at an average of almost one a game, including 97 in 111 internationals – more than twice as many as anyone else. I'd be proud of

that! Not bad when you consider he struggled with a knee injury most of his long career. He's also the only player to have won three World Cup winners' medals – in '58 (scoring twice in the Final as a seventeen-year-old), '62 and '70. Born into poverty, Pelé's rise to fame and fortune is a real fairy tale. Even a war in Nigeria was stopped for a two-day truce so that both armies could watch him in action.

They are my top two stars of all-time, but the third must be **Alfredo Di Stefano** who played for both Argentina and Spain and who was the idol of the young Johan himself. There can be no greater praise than that as far as I'm concerned. Di Stefano was possibly the greatest all-round forward of his generation and dominated European football in the 1950s and early 60s. He inspired the legendary Real Madrid side to win the European Cup five seasons on the trot from 1956, scoring in every Final and claiming a hat-trick in Real's 7–3 demolition of Eintracht Frankfurt in the last one at Hampden Park, Glasgow, in 1960. His strike partner, the tubby Hungarian with the lethal left foot, **Ferenc Puskas**, grabbed the other four goals in what some people say was the greatest football match ever. What a

pair Di Stefano and Puskas were! Puskas got another hat-trick in the '62 Final and scored an incredible 83 goals in 84 internationals.

Like most great players, Di Stefano worked hard, too, and had tremendous stamina as well as super ball skills. Another player with all those qualities was an Englishman, the late, great **Duncan Edwards** who was tragically killed, aged only 21, in the Munich air disaster in 1958. If Edwards had survived the plane crash, like Bobby Charlton, then he might well have been the England captain to lift the World Cup trophy eight years later.

Did you know there's been a survey on the Internet to allow thousands of football fans to vote for their favourite old stars? Their choices were whittled down to twenty-five names by sports-writers for a Hall of Fame Soccer Museum, but they were so biased that six of the top ten were British – ridiculous! And what made it even crazier was that Johan was only at number four!!! Can you believe that? For the record, the first ten on the list were: Pelé; George Best; Bobby Charlton; Johan Cruyff; Bobby Moore; Gordon Banks; Marco Van Basten; Franz Beckenbauer; John Charles; Kenny

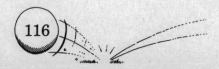

Dalglish; with Duncan Edwards next. It's about time somebody like me redressed the balance. My own top ten that follows is much fairer because I'm only choosing one player per country.

1. Johan Cruyff (Holland)
2. Pelé (Brazil)
3. Alfredo Di Stefano (Argentina & Spain)
4. Franz Beckenbauer (West Germany)
5. Bobby Charlton (England)
6. George Best (Northern Ireland)
7. Ferenc Puskas (Hungary)
8. Eusebio (Portugal)
9. John Charles (Wales)
10. Denis Law (Scotland)

What a team they would have made! In fact, I tried to make a team out of them before realizing I'd only got a couple of defenders. I suppose that's my own bias showing through as a striker myself. But nobody would beat that lot, even so. They'd always score more goals than they let in. I would, however, also need a star goalie to make up the eleven, and my choice for that key position would be the huge

**Lev Yashin** (The Black Panther) of the Soviet Union, as Russia was called in his days. I'm going to save writing about goalkeepers for another time. As my Swifts' teammate Sanjay says, they deserve a special piece all to themselves.

Let me just give you a potted biography of the other players I picked:

* **Franz Beckenbauer**: stylish, unflappable defender who more or less invented the modern, attacking sweeper role for club and country. Won the European Cup three times in a row in the 70s with Bayern Munich and also skippered West Germany to their '74 World Cup success. Coached them to victory in 1990 too.

* **Bobby Charlton**, now Sir Bobby: most famous English footballer with a record 49 goals for his country, one more than Gary Lineker. Cannonball shot with either foot; scored twice to help Manchester United win the European Cup in '68 and a vital member of the '66 World Cup winning England team. Such a modest superstar!

* **George Best**: not modest at all, but a teammate of Charlton and Law in the great United sides of

the 60s. What a fantastic trio they made! Had a pop star image and was perhaps the most naturally gifted British player of the modern era, so quick and skilful. Sadly, his personal problems off the field forced his early retirement.

* **Denis Law** (The King): great goalscorer (over 300 goals) and crowd-pleaser for his bravery, fiery temperament and cheeky grin. Bought by United in '62 for British record transfer fee of £115,000. Wouldn't have bought his big toe these days, would it?

* **Eusebio** (Ferreira Da Silva): first African player to earn a worldwide reputation, great sportsman and goalscorer for Benfica and Portugal. Top scorer in '66 World Cup with nine goals. Emotional, popular player – burst into tears more easily than Gazza!

* **John Charles**: star for Leeds, Juventus, Cardiff and Wales in 50s and 60s at centre-half or centre-forward. Known as the Gentle Giant in Italy where he's still a legend after scoring 93 goals and winning three championships in five seasons with Juventus. Big, strong, powerful man who never got booked or sent off!

Well, that's just about it, I guess. No space left to tell you anything about all the many great players I've reluctantly had to leave out. Fancy having no room to include such magnificent old stars as the ice-cool captain **Bobby Moore**; the sensational, controversial **Diego Maradona**; the 'Wizard of the Dribble' **Sir Stanley Matthews**; the Scottish cult hero **'Slim Jim' Baxter**; the 'Preston Plumber' **Sir Tom Finney**; the German goal-machine **Gerd Müller**; the battling England captain **Billy Wright**; the elegant, intelligent **Danny Blanchflower**; the skilful Frenchman **Michel Platini**; the three 'R's of Italian folklore **Riva, Rivera & Rossi**; and enough exciting Brazilians to beat the Rest of the World on their own! And that's not to mention all the soccer legends from the first half of the 20th century. I'd be at it for ever – and I've still got my school homework to do that's supposed to be handed in tomorrow.

I'll finish off by setting you a bit of enjoyable homework that you might like to try out with your mates sometime. Why don't you attempt to put together a team of outstanding modern players that could form a World XI to take on anybody in the Universe? Best to make that a squad, on second

thoughts, as you're bound to disagree and you'll probably need a few subs if some multi-limbed aliens start cutting up rough! But remember to make it a truly international squad with stars from all over the planet. Football's the *greatest* game in the whole wide world!

See ya!

*Luke*

# ROB CHILDS

# SOCCER SHOCKS

## Illustrated by Jon Riley

Corgi Yearling Books

*Especially for all soccer teachers and coaches*

# 1 Sweeper System

'Watch it! Here comes Tubs,' warned Sanjay from his goal. 'Better hide any choc you've got left.'

'Wonder how many eggs Tubs scoffed this Easter?' laughed Titch as the roly-poly defender waddled across the village recreation ground towards the group of footballers.

The goalkeeper grinned. 'Tons, I bet. He's even shaped like one.'

Luke Crawford glanced at the time. 'C'mon, Tubs, you should've been here a quarter of an hour ago,' he called out, trying to exert his non-existent authority as captain. 'What's kept you?'

Tubs didn't respond till he reached the pitch

and leant on the goalpost, which creaked and shifted under his weight. 'Dinner,' he grunted.

'Careful, Tubs!' cried Sanjay, supporting the woodwork. 'I need my goal in one piece for Sunday's game.'

'Huh! Pity you don't protect it better during matches,' he snorted, giving the post a sly kick before moving away.

'You can be on my side,' Luke decided. 'We're a man short.'

'Yeah, I've seen Titch,' Tubs smirked. 'But where's the rest of 'em?'

'Thought Ricki was supposed to be here today as well,' Sanjay put in, gazing into the distance where the Garner twins were battling for possession of the ball. The other players had taken the chance to slump onto the ground, content to wait until either Gary or Gregg returned in triumph.

'So did I,' Luke admitted. 'I rang Ricki up a couple of days ago to remind him about the practice. Said I'd got big plans for him.'

Tubs let out his rumbling laugh. 'Well, that explains it, then. Your cousin's got more sense than I gave him credit. He knows when it's best to stay away.'

Privately, Luke was quite encouraged that so many of his squad had bothered to turn up for training in the school holidays. He liked to think it showed their commitment to playing for Swillsby Swifts, the under-13 Sunday League team of soccer misfits that he'd formed at the start of the season. Running his own team was the only way that Luke could guarantee himself a regular game of football.

'Er . . . what exactly are these big plans of yours, anyway?' asked Sanjay warily. 'Isn't it a bit late to start devising new tactics?'

'Never too late for making improvements,' Luke beamed. 'We've got to make sure we pick

up the extra points we need to steer clear of relegation.'

'And how many more do we need, d'yer reckon?'

Luke was usually vague – or evasive – on this touchy subject, making sure the other players never saw the updated league table that he received in the post every week. He gave a little shrug. 'Not many.'

'How many?' Tubs insisted.

'Look out!' Sanjay yelled. 'Here he comes.'

'Who?' demanded Titch. 'Friend or foe?'

'How should I know?' replied the goalkeeper as one of the twins ran towards them. 'Just go and stop him.'

'He might be on my side.'

'He *is* on your side,' Luke told him. 'It's Gary.'

Titch was impressed. 'How d'yer know that?'

'Gary's got a left foot. Look at the way he dribbles with it. Gregg only uses *his* left to fill the other boot.'

'Well, don't just give him a free shot at goal, whoever he is,' Sanjay kept on. 'Somebody go and get in his way.'

Tubs took the instruction literally. He'd found from experience that the best method of dealing with fast, tricky opponents was simply to stand in their way. So that's what he did. He positioned

himself right in Gary's flightpath and nobody
blocked the route to goal better than Tubs. Head
down, the onrushing Gary cannoned into Tubs
at full throttle and bounced away as if from the
cushion of a snooker table.

The ball ran loose to Luke and the skipper
broke into his habitual commentary mode to
describe – or at least interpret – the ensuing
action.

'. . . *And now the Swifts player-manager, Luke
Crawford, moves smoothly on to the ball . . .*' (he
trod on it and stumbled)

'. . . *and finds himself on his own with no support* . . .' (everyone else was watching – and listening – with amusement)

'. . . *the skipper dummies one way and then the other to wrong-foot the defence* . . .' (he and the ball went in different directions)

'. . . *and then cuts inside onto his trusty right foot* . . .' (both of his feet were about as trustworthy as leaving Tubs in charge of the school tuck shop)

'. . . *the striker looks up to see the goalie straying off his line and then coolly picks his spot* . . .' (Sanjay had moved to one side to give Luke the whole goal to aim at)

'. . . *chipping the ball over the keeper's head towards the top corner of the net* . . .' (he sliced it up into the air towards the far corner of the recky)

'. . . *and the crowd goes wild with delight* . . .' (the other players rolled about in uncontrolled hilarity as Luke charged after the stray ball, still broadcasting his own version of events to the world).

Ricki arrived half an hour later. He hadn't missed all that much action. His teammates were sprawled on the grass again, taking yet another breather.

133

'Sorry about time,' Ricki began, spreading his hands in a gesture of helplessness. 'My father is plenty mad – the car break down, y'know . . .'

'Don't worry about it, Ricki,' said Tubs. 'Crawford things never work properly.'

'My name is Fortuna,' Ricki corrected him. 'My father, he is Italian.'

'Yeah, we know that, but your mother's got no excuse. She comes with the family jinx.'

'*Jinx?* What is this jinx?'

'It's another word we have round here for Crawford.'

Luke gave Tubs a dirty look. 'Don't listen to him, Ricki,' he said. 'We're just glad to have you here.'

'Got bad news,' he said, squatting next to his cousin. 'My father says we must be going home soon.'

'But you've only just got here,' Luke protested. 'I want us to work on some new tactics before we pack up.'

'No, I mean really go home,' Ricki explained. 'To Roma.'

'What!' cried Luke, jumping to his feet in alarm. 'You *can't* do that. It's not the end of the season yet. We need you.'

'I am plenty sorry, Luke – I want to stay, y'know, but . . .'

Sanjay interrupted. 'You mean you'd rather play for the Swifts than go back to sunny Italy?' he said in disbelief. 'You must be as daft as the rest of the family after all!'

Luke decided the best way to relieve his frustrations, as always, was to kick a ball about. It didn't seem to matter too much that the ball rarely went where he intended, just so long as it *went* – and so that he could go and miskick it again somewhere else.

'C'mon, you lot, on your feet,' he called out. 'We've got work to do.'

There were grumbles all round.

'Aw, Skipper, I was just gettin' comfy,' complained Dazza, whom Luke had been trying unsuccessfully to convert from winger to wing-back.

'Yeah, we've done enough running about for one day,' said Tubs.

Luke tried to haul Tubs to his feet, but quickly realized that was a waste of effort. He'd need a crane to help him. 'You haven't done any running about yet, Tubs,' he pointed out. 'You never do.'

Tubs' full-moon face creased up. 'That's my motto,' he chuckled. 'Don't run before you can walk.'

Eventually, under protest, the players stirred

themselves and let Luke explain his latest plans. The Swifts had changed their tactical formations this season more times than Tubs broke into a sweat during a game.

'We're going to use a sweeper system in our next match, I've got it all worked out,' Luke gabbled. 'And Ricki here is going to be our sweeper.'

Ricki looked as puzzled as the rest. 'Me, sweeper?' he queried. 'You mean I need a brush?'

'Only to clear up the plenty big mess we're in,' Tubs grunted.

Luke ignored the jibe. 'No, it means I want you to play deeper than usual, behind the main markers, dealing with anything that gets past them.'

'Who are our main markers?' put in Sanjay. 'I didn't know we had any.'

'Ha! Ha! Very funny,' retorted Big Ben, their centre-back, pretending to look hurt. 'It's about time we had a bit of extra help in defence.'

'You'll soon see how it works, Ricki,' Luke assured him. 'Just stay back and cover the others, OK? Put yourself about plenty.'

'Ah, got it. I put myself about plenty good. I like the sound of that.'

Ricki scampered around like a playful puppy in the short session that followed, eager to

please, but he rarely popped up in the places Luke wanted him to be – that is, wherever the ball was.

'I try my best, Luke, yes?' Ricki said. 'It's just that rugby is my game, you know that. I not really understand soccer rules.'

'Join the club, Ricki, old mate,' chortled Tubs. 'Neither do we.'

The practice fizzled out after the Garner twins had to go home early and Titch also made an excuse to leave.

'Got to take my goldfish out for a walk,' he said before trailing away.

'Big game on Sunday,' Luke reminded the others. 'Vital league points at stake.'

'Who we playing?' asked Brain.

'Don't you ever read the fixture book?' Luke replied, then realized who had spoken. Brian Draper, the Swifts' one truly talented player, didn't read anything unless he had to, due to his dyslexic difficulties. 'Sorry, Brain, it's a home match here against Southcote United. Two o'clock kick-off.'

'How many did we lose by at their place?' asked Dazza.

'Who said we lost?'

'Just take it for granted. So what was the score, then?'

Luke mumbled something that no-one heard.

'Er, sorry, Skipper,' smirked Big Ben. 'Didn't quite catch that.'

'Um . . . I'll have to check,' Luke said, pretending to be untying his laces.

'Rubbish!' exclaimed Tubs. 'You know all the results off by heart. You've got 'em logged in that little black book of yours.'

How the other players would love to get hold of that record book! They knew Luke used it to keep not only the statistical details of every match, but also to write up fanciful reports of his own contributions to the action.

'Double figures, I bet,' grinned Dazza. 'The only time the skipper ever goes quiet is when he's asked about the scores.'

'It wasn't double figures, if you must know,' Luke sneered. 'It was only seven.'

'Oh, well, that's all right, then. They must have hit us on a good day.'

'Well, they won't even know what's hit *them* this time,' Luke said with determination. 'We've improved loads since that first meeting.'

Tubs let out a loud guffaw. 'Save the fiction for your little black book, Skipper. We're gonna get thrashed again, admit it. We don't mind.'

'No, we won't,' said Luke, standing up, his face flushed. 'Not with our new sweeper system in operation. They won't be able to work that out.'

'Well, that'll make things fair, then,' Tubs grinned. ''Cos nor can we!'

## 2 Distractions

The match against Southcote United may well have kicked off in the afternoon, but the Swifts still managed to look half asleep.

United shook the home side roughly out of their slumbers with a goal in the very first minute and soon grabbed another from a corner. The only times Sanjay had been able to get his hands on the ball was when he bent to pick it out of the net.

'Wake up!' cried Luke's father. 'You're letting them walk all over us.'

'No change there, then,' murmured Uncle Ray, taking off his glasses to wipe them. 'Teams have been using us as a doormat all season.'

'I shouldn't put your specs back on, if I were you,' said his brother. 'Things may not look quite so bad without them.'

'I won't be able to see a thing.'

'Exactly! Lucky you.'

The Crawford brothers were officially in charge of the Swifts, having their names in the league handbook as manager and secretary, but that was only for form's sake – or for the work of filling in forms. They left all the coaching to the skipper. In theory, at least, Luke was in full control. In practice, and even more so in games, things were invariably out of control.

'C'mon, defence, sort out the marking,' the player-manager complained. 'Who's supposed to be picking up that big number eight at corners?'

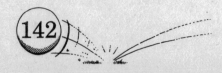

The defenders looked round at each other, hoping somebody else might be willing to take the blame. Nobody was. They were all far better at passing the buck than passing the ball.

'Thought the sweeper was gonna take care of anybody who's free,' grumbled Tubs. 'He's our spare man.'

'There were two Reds,' Ricki protested. 'I cannot mark both.'

'Shame how you chose the wrong one,' Tubs retorted.

Any intended irony was wasted on Ricki. It went right over his head, much like the ball had done.

Despite the poor start, Luke was prepared to be more tolerant. He wanted to give his new system every chance to be a success before it was thrown onto the Swifts' ever-growing tactical scrapheap.

Luke gave Ricki a slap on the back in encouragement. 'Not your fault,' he said. 'Bound to be a few teething troubles at first.'

'Teething troubles?' Ricki repeated.

'Um . . . yeah, y'know, like a baby has,' Luke replied hesitantly, sensing that Ricki would still have no idea what he was trying to say. 'Um . . . you can't expect things to work out right straightaway. Needs time . . .'

143

Time was just one crucial factor the Swifts did not have in their favour, either in this match or in what little was left of the season. Another was skill – a vital commodity also in very short supply in the Swifts' changing room, and even more obviously missing out on the pitch.

After such a flying start, United may have been guilty of coasting and only scored once more before the interval. And with their minds perhaps on the half-time refreshments, they even allowed the Swifts to pull a goal back. The visitors defended a corner sloppily, letting the ball skid right through the penalty area to an opponent lurking near the right touchline.

The main reason Tubs was there was to be the nearest to the trays of orange segments when the whistle blew. Annoyed by the distraction from the food, he lashed the ball back across the area where it was met by a spectacular diving header.

Ricki had arrived late, unnoticed, to join the attack and threw himself forward at the leather missile. Only at the last split second did he head it rather than make a rugby-style catch. The ball thudded against the far post and Dazza gleefully lashed the rebound high into the roof of the net.

'*GOAL!!*' screamed the player-commentator. '*What a time to score! It's only 3–1 now and there's no doubt who will enjoy the oranges more during the break – they're bound to taste all the sweeter to the Swifts . . .*'

Tubs could already tell everyone how sweet they were. He celebrated the goal by helping himself from one of the trays.

'OK, men, listen,' said Luke. 'I reckon it's just a matter of time before we score another goal. We've got them rattled, I can tell . . .'

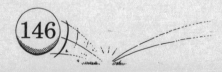

Luke trailed off, realizing he was talking to himself. His teammates' attention was fixed elsewhere and even the few remaining scraps of orange lay neglected on the ground.

'Who's that?'

'Dunno – never seen her before.'

'Must be with one of the Southcote mob.'

'Doubt it. She's heading straight for us.'

To the boys' astonishment, the girl in question was walking across the pitch and they instinctively huddled closer together for protection.

'What's she want with us?'

'Perhaps she's after our autographs?'

'She doesn't look that stupid.'

Ricki gave a little nervous cough. 'Um . . . sorry, you guys,' he faltered, beginning to redden. 'She is sort of with me, y'know.'

They stared at him with a mixture of new respect and suspicion.

'She from Italy, as well, then?' asked Gary.

'Um . . . no, she is in my class at school in Padley,' Ricki explained. 'She is giving me extra help with my English, see?'

Tubs nodded, his chins wobbling in agreement.

'I see, all right,' he said, giving Ricki a leer. 'She must be plenty good, yes?'

The boys were still laughing as the girl reached the group. 'Hi!' she greeted them confidently. Is the game over?'

'It is for us just about,' muttered Big Ben.

'No, it's not,' Luke stated defiantly. 'We're right back in it now and . . .'

The skipper was interrupted as usual, but this was the first time that his attempted team talk had been stalled by a girl.

'You must be Luke,' she said, failing to hide a smirk.

'Amazing!' gasped Sanjay. 'Your fame's spreading, Skipper. You're even getting recognized now.'

'Ricki's told me all about you,' she smiled, making Luke blush too.

'Soz, the skipper doesn't sign autographs till after the match,' said Gary, sidling up to her. 'Er, didn't catch your name . . .'

'It's Laura. Mind if I borrow Ricki for a minute?'

'So long as you let us have him back for the second half. He's our sweeper.'

'Sweeper?'

'Yeah, don't worry about it,' Gary grinned. 'None of us really understands what it means, either.'

Laura led an embarrassed Ricki a little distance away but, try as they might, his teammates could not overhear what was being said.

'What's she after?' grunted Mark, the centre-back. 'Hasn't Ricki done his homework or something?'

'She can keep me behind after school any time,' Gary grinned, nudging his twin. 'How about you, Junior?'

Gregg pulled a face. He didn't like it when Gary used that pet nickname to emphasize the ten minutes' seniority that Gary claimed over him.

'I wouldn't know,' Gregg replied sourly. 'I haven't got your experience.'

The referee's whistle cut short any further speculation and half-time ended without Luke having been able to make any of the coaching points he'd considered vital. But that was normal, anyway. The players always seemed to find something else of greater interest to distract them.

'C'mon, Ricki!' Luke called out in frustration.

'Time's up, number four, come on in,' chortled Tubs. 'Business before pleasure.'

As Laura went to stand on the touchline, the Swifts refused to budge until Ricki rejoined them.

'Well?' demanded Mark.

'Well what?' said Ricki.

'What did she want?'

The referee gave another impatient beep.

'C'mon, men!' Luke urged. 'We've got work to do. We can still win this game.'

'Belt up, Skipper, this is important,' said Tubs. 'C'mon, Ricki – spill the beans.'

Ricki looked blank. 'Spill the beans?'

'Oh, ignore Tubs, he's always going on about food,' grinned Gary. 'Just tell us what your friend Laura had to say.'

'She has invited me to her home for tea,' he explained. 'Her parents, they want to meet me.'

'Bet Tubs wishes he could meet a girl like that, inviting him for tea on their first date,' joked Sanjay.

''Fraid you've had it now, mate,' said Gary, draping an arm around Ricki in mock consolation.

'Why is that?'

'It's an old English custom of ours,' he replied,

trying hard to keep a straight face. 'Getting invited to meet the folks is just the first step.'

'First step?'

'Yeah – towards getting married!' Gary exclaimed. 'Congratulations!'

# 3 Party-Poopers

The Swifts played the second half with the equivalent of ten and a half men – nine and a half if you discounted the skipper, which was usually wise.

Ricki was mentally absent and Luke, well, Luke was just mental. The other players were made aware of Luke's physical presence by an irritating droning noise in their ears – his running commentary on the game that was swirling around him.

*'With their sweeper having gone walkabout upfield, the skipper now has to fill in for the wandering star, sacrificing himself for the good of the team. Fortuna's way out of position as a*

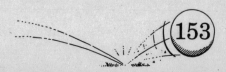

*Swifts attack breaks down and the red shirts of United surge forward once more. The winger races past Gary Garner and cuts into the box, but the skipper glides across to intercept and plug the gap. He times his tackle to perfection . . . aaahhh!'*

'Penalty!' went up the United chorus as the winger sprawled full-length over Luke's outstretched leg.

'Huh! Nice one, Skipper!' groaned Sanjay, as the referee pointed to the penalty spot. 'That's a real big help.'

The goalkeeper had been in this one-against-one situation many times during the course of the season. With a heavy sigh of resignation, he positioned himself on his line, mercifully out of reception range of Luke's on-going description of the scene from the edge of the penalty area.

*'. . . and the kicker runs confidently in, doing a little jink in his curved approach to try and fool the keeper. He blasts the ball and – oh! It struck the post and rebounded into the keeper's arms. Sanjay Mistry never even made a move for the ball. Just the kind of break the plucky Swifts deserve . . .'*

Sanjay hoofed the ball away upfield, but his relief was only temporary. The ball was lobbed straight back into the goalmouth to the very boy who had just missed the penalty and he took

immediate revenge by smacking it past the help-
less Sanjay.

*Peeeeeppppp!!*

*'No goal!'* cried the commentator. *'The ref's
disallowed it for offside. Thanks to the skipper's
quick thinking, he's saved his team from falling
further behind. The emergency sweeper urged his
defence to move out after the penalty drama and
the striker was caught in their well-practised
offside trap . . .'*

The reality, as always, was somewhat
different. The Swifts defenders wouldn't recognize an offside trap if it sprang up and bit
them on the nose. Fortune, if not Fortuna, was

smiling on them for once. The Reds striker had been too busy sulking after his miss and had mooched away from goal even slower than Tubs. He was now doubly guilty of letting the Swifts off the hook.

Five minutes later, the Swifts made him feel even worse. The Garner twins linked up almost telepathically in midfield, playing a neat one-two exchange that sent Gregg galloping goalwards. He rather went and spoiled things by tripping over outside the penalty area, but the ball ran free to Brain who cut in from the left wing to shoot home with a right-foot drive.

*'3–2! The Swifts fightback has sure got the United players worried. You can see it in their body language. They know they've got a real match on their hands now. Their faces look strained, their shoulders have slumped, their legs are feeling like lead and their hearts must be pounding . . .'*

Given the opportunity, the commentator might well have worked his way through most of the opposition's body parts – including the rude bits – but his attention was caught by a commotion on the touchline. Ricki seemed to have got himself involved in a brawl.

'You want to get yourself sent off?' cried Big Ben, who was helping to drag Ricki away. 'What d'yer think you're doing?'

'These two,' Ricki protested, jabbing an accusing finger at the United substitutes. 'They pester Laura.'

'I could have dealt with them myself, thanks,' she said hotly. 'You've only gone and made things worse.'

Big Ben guided the crestfallen Ricki back onto the pitch. 'C'mon, this is no time to play the gallant Latin lover,' he said. 'You're supposed to be playing football.'

'See you after the match, yes?' Ricki called to her.

Laura shook her head. 'No, I have to get back home now. Dad's waiting in the car. See you at the party later, OK?'

'Party?' repeated Big Ben. 'Thought you said it was just for tea.'

Ricki shrugged. 'She not want to invite all of you as well.'

'Charming! She didn't want any riff-raff, is that it?'

'Riff-raff?'

'Yeah, like us Swifts,' explained Tubs. 'Can't say I blame her really.'

'We're not riff-raff,' Luke objected. 'If anybody treats us like that, they're in for a shock. Look at United. They're all getting at each other now, panicking 'cos they know we can beat 'em.'

'More like Dis-United!' joked Titch.

'Right, let's go for that equalizer, team,' cried Luke, rallying his forces. 'And then the winner!'

To give the Swifts due credit, they did try their best and went close to scoring an all-important third goal, one that might well have led to them snatching all three precious points. A shot from Gregg skimmed just wide of a post and the goalie was fortunate in blocking Brain's volley with his legs. Sadly, however, that was about as good as it got.

The visitors managed to rally their forces and

put the match effectively beyond reach with an
excellent fourth goal. Only two fine saves from
Sanjay near the end prevented United from adding further to their tally, but the Swifts were far
from downhearted. The players knew they'd
given a good account of themselves, despite the
final result.

'Never mind, Skip, we nearly did it,' said Dazza
as they trooped off the pitch. 'At least you'll be
able to give us a good write-up now in that little
black book of yours.'

Dazza giggled and headed for the changing
cabin, leaving the player-manager to ponder
over what might have been.

'Nearly's not good enough,' he sighed. 'You don't get any points for *nearly*. That's why we're down at the bottom of the table.'

Before tea, Luke went to his room to bring his personal record book up to date. Personal, because the exaggerated accounts of his performances were meant for *his* eyes only, and also because hardly anybody else normally managed to get a mention. He could make any defeat, no matter how catastrophic, sound almost like a

victory. United were very lucky, in this book, even to end up winning.

Luke had to be a little more circumspect, if not exactly accurate, in his next piece of sports reporting. This was more for public consumption, if anybody else apart from his teammates ever bothered to read it.

Uncle Ray was the editor of the village's free newspaper, the *Swillsby Chronicle*, and allowed Luke space for match reports – often testing Ray's editorial skills to the limit in deciding how much of Luke's biased and semi-fictional prose could actually be printed.

It was a task that Luke loved, even if he did regret that he could rarely report on a Swifts triumph. He scribbled a few thoughts down on a piece of notepaper then settled himself at the keyboard of his computer.

## So Near, Yet So Far

*by our soccer correspondent*

### Swillsby Swifts 2 – 4 Southcote United

The Swifts player-manager Luke Crawford described this setback as the win-that-got-away. His team showed great spirit after falling

behind to early goals and deserved at least a point to help their crusade against relegation.

'Our new sweeper system still needs a little bit more fine-tuning to work smoothly,' the coach admitted, 'but the lads are confident they can put things right before their next key fixture.'

Strikes from David 'Dazza' Richards and Brian 'Brain' Draper brought the battling Swifts right back into this match, but a crowd disturbance proved something of a distraction and United managed to hang on to their slim lead.

'Don't write us off yet,' said the skipper. 'The party isn't over till the man in black blows the final whistle! We will survive!'

# 4 Summer Term

'Wonder what all that noise is?' said Gary as he and Sean strolled past the P.E. shed at lunchtime on the first day of term.

'Dunno, and I don't care,' replied Sean, throwing his crisps packet down onto the playground.

'What's the matter with you? You sound as grumpy as old Frosty.'

'School! That's what's the matter with me. Having to come back to this dump when I could still be lying in bed like in the holidays.'

'Frosty' Winter, head of Swillsby Comprehensive's P.E. Department, suddenly emerged from the shed, brushing off the remains of a cobweb

from his hair. Gary gulped, hoping the teacher hadn't overheard his remark.

'You two!' Frosty barked. 'Come here.'

'It wasn't me, sir,' Gary said guiltily.

'What wasn't you?'

'Um . . . whatever you think I might have done, sir.'

Frosty sighed. 'That's your new policy, is it . . . er . . . ?' he began before stalling. He still couldn't tell the difference between the Garner twins, even at close quarters.

'He's Gregg, sir,' Sean put in helpfully, just in case Gary was going to get blamed for something.

'I knew that, thank you,' Frosty replied tetchily. 'It's your new policy, is it, Gregg, to deny something even before you've been accused? You're as bad as your brother.'

Gary wasn't sure whether or not to take that as a compliment. 'Oh, I'm not as bad as all that, sir,' he said innocently.

Frosty couldn't be bothered to pursue the matter. 'Come in here, both of you,' he ordered. 'I've got a job for you.'

The boys groaned inwardly. By the state of Frosty's tracksuit, it looked like it might well be a very dirty job. Sean was especially displeased. He prided himself on his immaculate appearance.

'Oh, and Sean . . .' Frosty added over his shoulder as he led the way in.

'Yes, sir,' replied Sean eagerly, hoping he might be given something else – less messy – to do instead.

'. . . Pick up that crisps packet first that you just dropped.'

The teacher had been struggling to sort out the sports equipment that would be needed in the new term. Sets of cricket stumps, bats and pads, many with buckles missing, were strewn over the shed floor along with javelins, discuses, shot puts, tape measures and relay batons.

Sean eyed the dirty pads with distaste. 'Don't fancy wearing any of them,' he muttered. 'Looks like something's been chewing them.'

'They were already like that last year,' said Gary.

'Aye, and they'll be like that next year too,' rasped Frosty. 'School can't afford to buy new ones. C'mon, give me a hand with these things.'

Frosty began to haul at sets of hurdles, cursing under his breath as they kept getting trapped by each other and by other pieces of apparatus.

'Some fool just chucked 'em in here at the end of last summer and didn't bother to stack them properly,' he muttered by way of explanation. 'Thank God it's the last time I'll have to do this chore.'

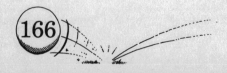

The boys glanced at each other. 'Er . . . why's that, sir?' asked Gary.

Frosty forced two hurdles apart. 'Oh, nothing,' he replied, trying to pass it off. 'Put this lot outside and make more room for all the cricket stuff.'

'What d'yer reckon?' hissed Gary as they propped the hurdles on the grass.

'I reckon it's about time old Frosty learnt to say *please*,' Sean grumbled, picking a piece of dirt off his trousers. 'These things are filthy.'

'Never mind them. I mean, about what he just said – about this being the last time?'

Sean gave a little shrug. 'Who knows? Maybe he's gonna store them somewhere else.'

'Don't be a moron. That was just an excuse.'

'So what? Let's just shift the hurdles and perhaps he'll let us go then.'

'Got a feeling it might just be Frosty who's going.'

'How d'yer mean?'

'Well, y'know – leaving or something.'

Sean pulled a face. 'More like retiring, if you ask me. He must be at least a hundred!'

Their speculation was cut short. 'Oi! C'mon, you two – get a move on,' thundered a voice from deep inside the shed. 'I don't want to be here for ever.'

It was a time in schools when the seasons overlapped for a short while. Goalposts stayed up long enough to play any outstanding soccer matches, but there were also the conflicting interests of summer sports like cricket and athletics that demanded space on the playing fields.

Frosty wanted the football finished and out of the way as soon as possible. The under-13s had somehow managed to reach the Final of the local cup competition, despite the fact that over half the team was now made up of Swifts. Many other – better – players had been driven away by Frosty's bad temper and sarcasm.

*Frostbite*, as it was known, had recently claimed the Year 8 captain, Matthew Clarke, as its most notable victim, but it seemed to have little effect on the Swifts players who had grown more thick-skinned over the course of the season. Whatever they lacked in ability, they perhaps made up for to some extent in their enthusiasm for the game.

The skipper's armband had passed to Jon Crawford, Luke's talented cousin, who showed that he at least was on good form in a hastily arranged practice match against the Comp's Year 7 squad.

'*Johan's on the ball now,*' warbled Luke into his pretend microphone, a water bottle, as Jon broke free along the right wing. '*The defender's given him too much room, something I'm sure he's going to regret . . .*'

Even if the younger boy had been able to pick up Luke's touchline ramblings, he probably wouldn't have been aware that the pet nickname referred to a soccer legend who graced the game before any of them were born – Luke's hero, the great Dutch star of the 1970s, Johan Cruyff.

'*. . . Johan takes the full-back on at pace and sweeps past him as if he didn't exist. I doubt if the poor kid even knows where he's gone . . .*'

The new captain shaped to shoot as he reached the edge of the area, wrong-footing the keeper, but then slid the ball square to Brain instead to give his teammate the honour of drilling it low into the net.

'Good goal, lads,' Frosty called out, letting slip a piece of rare praise in recognition of the fact that the two players were his side's potential match-winners in the Final. In reality, they were the Comp's only hope of avoiding a heavy defeat against Grimthorpe School, who had already beaten them twice in the league.

The goal equalized the Year 7 team's opener when a long-distance shot had bobbled over Sanjay's ill-timed dive, and it soon paved the way for two more to give the older lads a deserved 3–1 advantage at half-time.

'Change ends quick,' Frosty bellowed. 'I want to get home soon.'

'Are we going to use any subs, sir?' asked Jon.

The teacher didn't need to follow his captain's gaze towards the touchline. He knew exactly to whom Jon was referring. 'Oh, I don't think we need to take such drastic measures yet, do you?' he said.

'It's only a practice, sir. You know how keen he is to get on the pitch.'

'Aye, I still have nightmares about it,' the

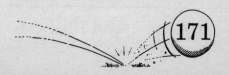

teacher grunted, attempting a piece of gruff humour. 'Oh, go on, then. If you want to – what do I care now?'

Jon gave his cousin a wave and Luke was pulling off his tracksuit top in an instant. Unfortunately, he'd forgotten that he still had the bottle in his hand and it got stuck halfway up his sleeve. The restart had to be delayed while the twins helped Luke to escape without breaking his arm.

'Who's going off, sir?' Luke asked as he ran on, his thin face flushed with excitement.

'Nobody.'

'But that means we'll have twelve men, sir. Won't that be an unfair advantage?'

'Only in theory,' came back the retort.

The Year 7 players might have complained if it had been anybody else but Luke Crawford. His fame – or infamy – spread well beyond the confines of his own year group in the school.

Not being allotted any particular position, Luke took that as a licence to roam, something that he always did anyway.

*'The experienced substitute has been given a floating role, to help out where most needed, and he's soon in the thick of the action, tracking back into his own penalty area . . .'*

'Get out of there!' barked Frosty, cutting off Luke's mobile commentary in mid-sentence. 'I don't want to see you anywhere near your own goal – got it? Stay upfield and make a nuisance of yourself in their half instead.'

That was something at least that Luke was very good at, making a nuisance of himself on the football field – and not only because of his knack of getting in other people's way . . .

'. . . *Luke Crawford drifts back upfield, unnoticed, like a phantom in the night, ghosting into space . . .'* whined his commentary, '. . . *they*

*seek him here, they seek him there, they seek the unseen striker everywhere . . .'*

Unseen, perhaps, but certainly not unheard. By the end of the game, the breathless voice-over had driven almost everybody to distraction. The only compensation for Luke's teammates was that they won – partly thanks to hardly allowing the substitute a kick – and for the younger losers in giving the source of their irritation as many kicks as possible.

# 5  Unlucky Luke

'What do you mean, this will be your last game?'

Ricki gave a shrug. 'I am plenty sorry, Luke,' he replied. 'My father, he say we have to go back to Roma next week.'

'But he promised me you'd be here till the end of the season.'

'Plans change,' Ricki said as an excuse. 'It is to do with business, y'know . . .'

Luke opened his mouth to speak again, but no sound came out. He was beside himself with frustration. He took a wild swing instead at a nearby ball and toppled over clumsily onto his backside.

'Uuurrgghhhh!'

He'd put his right hand into something soft and sticky – and he didn't need three guesses that it would be extremely smelly too.

'That's disgusting!' he complained, holding out his hand as if it didn't belong to him. 'Why don't some people clean up after their dogs?'

'What's the matter, Skipper?' asked Sean. 'Taking a break already?'

Luke pulled a face. 'Just give me a hand up, will you?'

'Sure . . .'

Luke saw the instant look of horror as Sean snatched his hand away a split second after making contact. He'd never heard such a fluent

stream of abuse leave Sean's lips and immediately regretted his action.

'I'm sorry, Sean, really I am,' he tried to apologize as his teammate turned to run back to the changing cabin. 'I just didn't think . . .'

It was too late for apologies. Luke sighed and got to his feet, unaided. 'Have to go and get cleaned up, too, I guess,' he said, glancing at his cousin.

'He was plenty mad,' Ricki said. 'Better find him, I think, before he goes home.'

Luke couldn't afford to lose anybody else. He charged back to the cabin at full speed.

'Wow! Just look at that boy go,' chortled Tubs from the pitch.

Big Ben laughed. 'He must have got caught short!'

'He ought to go in for the one hundred metres on Sports Day.'

'What event you going to do, Tubs?'

'Shot put, if old Frosty will let me. You only have to shuffle a few steps across the circle and then bung the thing as far as you can.'

'There must be a bit more to it than that.'

'Not the way I do it,' Tubs smirked. 'I'll even cut out the steps if I can get away with it.'

The Swifts kicked a ball around aimlessly, much like they did in matches, while they

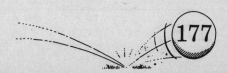

waited for the Saturday morning practice session to start. They certainly weren't going to exert themselves before their coach, captain and player-manager cajoled them into any purposeful action.

It was ten minutes before Luke, the holder of all these titles, eventually came out of the cabin with Sean trailing some way behind him. It had needed all Luke's powers of persuasion, promises, praise and pandering to Sean's ego before their stylish, left-footed midfielder grudgingly accepted his explanation that what happened had been accidental.

'Got it sorted, have you, Skipper?' Tubs laughed.

'Yeah, just a misunderstanding,' Luke claimed. 'We've shook hands on it now.'

'Trust you washed them first!' grinned Big Ben.

The session finally got under way and Luke did his best to inspire his depleted group of players to make the necessary effort. He almost took it for granted that not everybody would turn up. There were always a few missing, giving ever more fanciful excuses for their unavoidable absence.

'Big game here, tomorrow, men. We beat the Zebras away, remember – our first win of the season – and we need all three points again . . .'

Luke rarely managed to get through more than a couple of sentences before he was interrupted.

'What time's kick-off?' asked Sanjay.

'Half-past ten.'

'Can't we put it back a bit? Y'know, till the afternoon like some games.'

'We can't suddenly go changing things at the last minute,' Luke told him. 'Why do you want it later, anyway?'

'Got a big family get-together tonight. Could go on for ages.'

'Can't you tell them you need an early night?'

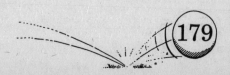

179

'It'll be too noisy. I wouldn't be able to get to sleep in any case.'

Luke sighed, wondering – not for the first time that season – why things were never simple. 'Just make sure you're here on time, Sanjay, OK? You were brilliant against the Zebras in that first game . . .'

'Yeah, at both ends!' put in Tubs. 'I'll never forget that header of yours.'

'Or the penalty save,' added Gary. 'Well wicked!'

'Right, you see how much we need you, Sanjay,' Luke continued, piling on the flattery. 'We beat this lot once, and we can do it again – but not without you.'

Sanjay lapped up the unaccustomed praise. 'Do my best, Skipper,' he beamed. 'Always do, you know that.'

'Could have fooled us,' murmured Big Ben, thinking of Sanjay's many howlers over the course of the season.

Sanjay was on top form during the brief session of attack versus defence that followed, keeping out goalbound shots from Brain, Gregg and Luke himself, much to the skipper's annoyance. It would have been a rare success for Luke, even in practice. Sanjay only let two goals in, a skimmer from Brain that eluded his grasp and

then an unintentional back-header from one of his own defenders that dropped underneath the crossbar.

'Just make sure you don't do one of them tomorrow, Big Ben,' Sanjay complained. 'Have enough problems with the opposition trying to get the ball past me, never mind all the own goal efforts from you-know-who.'

Big Ben grinned. 'You gonna be here, then, are you?'

'Course I am. You ain't got a chance without me around.'

It looked as if Sanjay's boast was going to be put to the test. The Swifts were sitting in the cabin,

already changed – or at least the ten players that had shown up – but there was still no sign of the goalkeeper.

'Can't keep the Zebras waiting any longer,' Luke decided. 'They're all out on the pitch, warming up.'

The skipper held up the team's spare goalie top. 'Er . . . any volunteers?'

'Tubs could go in goal, Skipper,' Gary suggested playfully. 'He'd fill most of it.'

Luke might have guessed there would be no serious takers. 'Right, then,' he said. 'Skipper's duty in a crisis. I'll wear it myself.'

It wasn't the first time that season Luke had been called into action as a stop-gap keeper. His technique tended to be more about gaps than stops, but he hadn't fared quite as badly as others feared. Apart from adding a few more embarrassing, if quite ingenious, own goals to his total, that is.

'Hey! Look!' cried one of the Zebras in delight as a green-clad Luke emerged from the cabin. 'That crazy Asian kid ain't in goal.'

'Magic! That gives us a better chance of beating them this time.'

'Dunno, maybe this kid's even better.'

'Doubt it. He's that weird captain of theirs. Don't reckon he could stop a bus.'

'Well, we'll soon see. Let's test him out early.'

The visitors did exactly that. The black and white striped Zebras, playing in an identical kit to that of the Comp, quickly capitalized on their double advantage of having an extra player on the pitch – and also of having Luke as the opposing keeper.

They swept straight through the middle and their centre-forward tried his luck with a shot from well outside the penalty area. Luke's dive was a textbook effort, but perhaps two pages of his manual on goalkeeping had stuck together – the bit about getting in the way of the ball seemed to have been overlooked. He had an

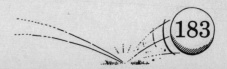

aerial view of the ball, too, as it passed beneath him, but his despairing glance backwards on landing showed him that it had also skidded wide of the post.

'Phew!' he sighed in relief. 'That was a close thing.'

Luke entrusted the goal-kick to the power of Tubs's mighty hoof, but he was called into action again immediately. With Tubs still out of position, the Zebras left-winger made the most of the huge amount of space that he now enjoyed as he dribbled goalwards. Confused by all the options available to him, the winger hit a hopeful centre-cum-shot that sailed beyond his team-mates and swirled towards the top left-hand corner of Luke's goal.

To his credit, Luke made a valiant effort to save it, but even the taller Sanjay would have been at full stretch to try and reach the ball. To his debit, however, when the ball ricocheted down from the angle of post and bar, Luke was still grounded and only succeeded in fumbling the ball over the line.

'Unlucky, Skipper!' cried Mark generously.

'Yeah, that just about sums me up,' he muttered under his breath. 'Unlucky Luke!'

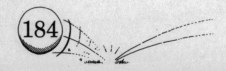

# 6 Ups and Downs

'Look! Here's Sanjay!' whooped Gary, pointing towards the car park.

Luke had sent Uncle Ray on an urgent errand of mercy to fetch Sanjay, even if the goalie had to be dragged out of bed. Fortunately, Sanjay was already in his goalie kit, not his pyjamas, and had been halfway to the ground when Ray screeched to a halt to give him a lift.

'Soz, overslept,' Sanjay called out. 'What's the score?'

'Losing 5–0!' Tubs bellowed back.

'What! You can't be – I'm not that late. Even Luke hasn't had time to let five in yet.'

'Course I haven't,' Luke protested. 'It's only two.'

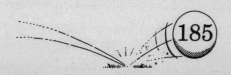

It was doubtful whether even Sanjay and Luke together would have prevented the second goal, a rasping close-range volley that tested how firmly the net pegs had been stuck in the soil.

Seeing Sanjay waiting impatiently to come on, the Zebras tried their best to keep the ball in play. They put together a long string of passes before the ball was teed up for the burly centre-forward to whack it goalwards. His arm was already raised in celebration when a green blur dived across his line of vision and turned the ball round the post.

'Great save!' yelled Mark.

'Wicked, Skipper!' grinned Dazza. 'Didn't know you had it in you.'

It was so rare for Luke to do something right on the football pitch that he appeared to forget all about Sanjay until the referee broke the spell.

'Well, are you going to bring on your other keeper or not?' he asked before allowing the corner to be taken. 'He's going bananas on the touchline.'

'Oh, yeah, right – suppose so,' Luke mumbled in a daze. He waved Sanjay on and somewhat reluctantly started to peel off the keeper's top to reveal his gold number nine shirt underneath.

The Swifts nearly conceded another goal straightaway. The corner was met by a soaring header and the ball clunked against the crossbar with a bang as loud as the farmer's bird-scarer device in the neighbouring field.

'. . . *That could be the turning point of the game,*' burbled the running – well, jogging – commentary as Luke traipsed upfield, feeling cold without his fleece-lined goalie top. '*Now that the Swifts are up to full-strength, there's every chance they can put the Zebras to flight . . .*'

There was indeed a definite shift in the balance of play. The Zebras lost their previous edge of confidence with the arrival of Sanjay, the scourge of their first encounter, and the Swifts hopes grew as they began to enjoy more possession in their opponents' half.

'Huh! Could have stayed in bed and caught up with my beauty sleep,' Sanjay grunted to himself. 'I've hardly touched the ball.'

Chances to score came and went, as they usually did, with Gregg guilty of the worst miss when he blazed over the bar from only two metres out. Just before half-time, however, the Swifts finally gained some reward for their efforts. Brain received a pass from Titch as he cut in from the wing, dribbled past a token challenge and steered the ball into the corner of the net.

'. . . *only 2–1 down now, and the Swifts are in with a good shout . . .*' burbled the match summary as the referee blew for the interval. '*After a few well-chosen words of inspiration from their player-manager during the break, they should be able to take this game by the scruff of the neck and . . .*'

Luke was suddenly yanked back by his shirt collar. 'Just shut it, you!' snarled the Zebras captain. 'I've had just about as much as I can

188

stand of your voice. If I hear one more peep out
of you in the second half, you'll get my size
seven boot right up your inbuilt microphone –
got it?'

Luke nodded and moved away to a safe
distance before risking a retort – and even then
the sound was turned right down low. *'Peep!'*

Luke put down his favourite red pen on the desk
and gazed at the page of his black notebook with
quiet satisfaction. It was filled with his neat,
small handwriting, portraying the events of the
morning's game against the Zebras.

'Not bad,' he murmured. 'Not bad at all, even though I say so myself.'

He was the only one who was going to say so. Not only because nobody else was allowed access to his private soccer diary, but also because it would be very unlikely for them to form the same opinion as to the quality of its prose. The writer did rather have a tendency to exaggerate the importance of his own role, glossing over any self-inflicted wounds.

Having described his goalkeeping exploits in lurid detail, Luke read over the final paragraphs again, basking in the reflected glory.

*The Swifts responded to their coach's half-time tactical talk and took his wise words to heart. Sweeper Ricardo Fortuna, their Italian import who was playing the last game of his loan spell in England, was given licence to Rome (geddit?) further forward and created the equalizer. He exchanged passes cleverly with the skipper in midfield before setting up a chance that even Dazza could not miss.*

*While the Swifts might have been tempted to settle for a draw, the player-manager drove them on in the quest for all three points in their battle against relegation. 'One point wouldn't have been enough,' Luke Crawford told reporters after the match. 'We had to throw caution to the wind.'*

This brave policy almost backfired when Sanjay was left exposed and raced off his line to save at an attacker's feet, but earned its reward a few minutes from the end. Ricki gave the Swifts a farewell present worth his weight in gold – or certainly in lira – when he stormed upfield to meet a cross and head the ball home. This gave the Swifts the double over the Zebras, winning both league encounters 3–2.

'Survival is now in our own hands,' said the skipper confidently. 'We won't go down without a fight.'

Luke stood up and paced the room in restless excitement. 'Two crunch games coming up,' he said aloud. 'What a way to end the season!'

Luke wasn't yet sure what part, if any, he might yet play in the first encounter, the Comp's Cup Final next Saturday morning. Frosty still hadn't named his team, but Luke remained hopeful he might be included. Like the Swifts, Frosty did not exactly have the luxury of a large squad to choose from.

'Be nice to win a medal,' Luke murmured dreamily and then broke out of his reverie. 'But it'd mean nothing if the Swifts went and got relegated next day. Can't let that happen – we just can't – not now . . .'

Big Ben's clearance upfield was punted too far ahead of the strikers and the ball bounced harmlessly out of play for a goal-kick.

'What kind of a pass was that meant to be?' complained Gregg. 'I'm not a greyhound, y'know.'

Big Ben grinned. 'No, but I reckoned the baby elephant in goal needed some exercise!'

Frosty let out a heavy sigh as he watched Tubs waddle after the ball. He guessed that the boy had only volunteered to have a go between the posts in this after-school practice to save doing any more running about.

'Anything wrong, sir?' came a voice behind him.

Frosty turned and gazed at Gary without apparent recognition.

'Um . . . it's just that you sounded a bit . . . like, fed up, sir, you know . . .'

'*Fed up?* I've been fed up for about the past twenty years,' the teacher growled as it began to drizzle. 'Fed up of being rained on, snowed on, blown about and half frozen to death – all for the sake of school sport.'

Gary glanced round, hoping that somebody might come and rescue him from such a torrent of self-pity. He was alone. To his credit, he attempted to fill the embarrassed silence between them.

'I'm sure it's not been all bad, sir,' he began, 'I mean, your teams must have won a few cups over the years – and we're in the Final on Saturday.'

'Oh, yes, how could I forget that?' Frosty retorted. 'I'm really looking forward to another public humiliation against Grimthorpe.'

At that very moment, Luke came trundling by, trying to dribble a ball. He found the triple combination of moving, ball control and commentating on his actions all too much. He stumbled over the ball and fell flat on his face.

Frosty caught Gary's eye and waved a dismissive arm around at the scene in general. 'It's Fate's last chance to kick old Frosty in the teeth,' he muttered, 'or at least what he's got left after grinding them all these years.'

Gary was so taken aback by Frosty using his own nickname that he almost missed the significance of the teacher's choice of words. 'Um . . . *last* chance, sir?' he repeated.

'Yes, last chance, boy,' he nodded, not even bothering to try and evade the issue. 'You might as well know. I was going to tell you all, anyway, after the Final. There seems to be a rumour

going round the school already, so it might as well be out in the open.'

'What's that, sir?' asked Gary, feigning innocence.

'I'm packing up at the end of term.'

Gary tried to look more shocked than pleased. 'Are you going to another school?'

'No, thank goodness. It's bad enough here. I'm retiring,' he admitted and then added, 'and that's *early* retirement I'm talking about, boy. I'm getting out while I've still got all my marbles left – and some of my hair!'

The rain started to come down harder. 'Right, you lot, we're going in,' Frosty shouted, pointing towards the school. 'I've had enough.'

# 7 Fire!

April was living up to its reputation for showers and the wind chill ensured that the temperature felt more like February. The weather was so bad that Luke was the only one who bothered to turn up at the rainswept recky for the Swifts midweek training session and even he stayed inside the changing cabin.

The skipper kept himself warm with an old single-bar electric fire and a solo game of football, using a tennis ball and one of the benches as a goal. Accompanied by his wild commentary, his frenetic, unco-ordinated actions were not a pretty sight – or sound – but no-one else was around to complain. This was doubly fortunate,

both for them and for him, as there were no witnesses as to who had broken the small pane of glass over the door.

Luke also found himself alone outside the school gates on Saturday morning, waiting to travel into the nearby town of Padley – the neutral venue for the Cup Final. Underneath his tracksuit and coat, Luke was wearing the black and white number thirteen shirt thrown to him (or at him) the previous day at the team meeting as the Comp's only available substitute.

'Might even give you that shirt as a farewell present,' Frosty had remarked gruffly, though with a little glint in his eye. 'Must be like an old friend to you by now.'

It was some while before anybody else showed up at the gates and Luke was relieved to see the Garner twins. He was beginning to think Frosty might have played some cruel joke on him and secretly arranged for the other players to gather somewhere else instead.

'Been here long, Luke?' asked Gregg, reserving his title of Skipper for Sundays.

'Bet he camped out all night,' chuckled Gary. 'Just to make sure we didn't leave without him.'

Luke took the usual banter in good heart. 'At least it's not raining yet this morning,' he said.

'Give it time,' muttered Mr Garner, eyeing the dark clouds overhead suspiciously.

Tubs was the next one to appear on the scene. His arrival was unexpected in the sense that he was running – or at least the nearest that Tubs would ever get to that unfamiliar form of locomotion. He rarely broke into anything more than a trot in an actual game.

'Hey! What's got into you, Tubs?' Gregg shouted. 'Where's the fire?'

It was some while before Tubs was in any state to answer. He looked shocked as well as out of breath. 'At the . . . recky!' he gasped, heaving.

'What d'yer mean, at the recky? What is?'

'The fire . . . you idiot!'

'What fire?' demanded Luke, suddenly concerned.

'The fire . . . that burnt down . . . the cabin!' Tubs managed to choke out.

Luke's cheeks, reddened by the wind, turned ghastly white as the blood drained from his face. 'Our cabin? Is this some kind of stupid joke?'

All of Tubs' spare flesh wobbled about as he vigorously shook his head in denial. 'Straight up . . . Luke . . .' he replied. 'Took a short cut . . . through the recky . . . to get here . . . and there it was . . . or wasn't. It's gone!'

'What! The cabin?'

'Yes! Are you deaf . . . as well as daft?' Tubs panted. 'Watch my lips – cabin is no more. Kaput – got it? All that's left are the front steps!'

Luke didn't take in very much of the first half. Not because the crowd was so great that he could barely get a view of the action – he could have stretched out along the touchline anywhere he liked – but because his mind kept drifting back to the recky.

Terrible pangs of guilt stabbed at Luke's conscience as he pictured the scene of devastation. 'Sure I switched that electric fire off when I left on Thursday,' he murmured to himself. 'Must have done.'

'Sorry I'm late,' said Dad, suddenly appearing at Luke's side and turning up his coat collar against the rain that was starting. 'Only I got called to the recky by the police. Guess you've already heard the bad news?'

He didn't need an answer. Luke's miserable face said it all.

'Cabin's totally gutted, I'm afraid,' Dad told him. 'Everything inside has been lost – nets, balls, the lot. Good job the posts were already set up on the pitch or they would've been barbecued too.'

'Um . . . how do they think it happened?' asked Luke hesitantly.

'They reckon it was vandals. I'd just like to get my hands on them, whoever they are.'

Luke gulped. 'What are we going to do about tomorrow's match?'

'Have to speak to Ray first. League rules say we must have nets on the posts for one thing – and a ball might perhaps come in useful too.'

Dad paused and nodded towards the pitch. 'What's the score here, then?' he asked. 'Have I missed much?'

Luke shrugged. 'Dunno – not really been watching.'

Dad was flabbergasted. 'Blimey! Things must be bad!' he gasped. 'If you can't keep track of how many Sanjay's let in, nobody can.'

At that moment, Jon received a pass on the halfway line and the next Grimthorpe player to touch the ball was the goalkeeper as he picked it out of the netting. Jon had treated the spectators to their first real glimpse of his special talents, taking the ball on a mazy run past several red shirts before chipping it teasingly over the advancing keeper.

'Great goal by our Jon, eh?' beamed Ray, trotting up to his brother. 'We're only 3–1 down now. That's really set the game alight . . .'

Ray realized what he'd just said and gave a little apologetic smile. 'Well, perhaps not the best way to put it in the circumstances.'

Luke sighed. Nobody would ever describe anything he did on the pitch in such glowing terms. Off the pitch, well, that was another matter . . .

'Luke! Luke!' came a shout. 'You're on.'

Luke was jolted out of his dark thoughts. He hadn't even bothered to go and join his teammates to receive Frosty's half-time tongue-lashing. He knew the teacher would at best ignore him or, at worst, insult him and he could do without suffering either indignity right now.

'C'mon, Luke!' Jon called out again. 'Get that coat off.'

Perhaps for the first time in his life – at least, ever since he'd been able to stand up – Luke wasn't in the mood for playing football. 'Typical!' he grunted. 'Trust old Frosty to go and make things even worse for me.'

'Good luck,' said Dad. 'Glad I got here in time to see you play. Go and show 'em how to do it.'

Luke forced a smile. He could *tell* them how something should be done all right, but even his dad knew there was no way in the world he could actually *show* them. He'd leave any practical

demonstrations to his cousin.

Frosty had already given up the game as lost and, to the captain's amazement, made no objection to Jon's suggestion that Luke might come on as an extra attacker.

Normally, Luke's natural enthusiasm would have over-ridden any instructions to stay in position and caused him to pop up in the unlikeliest of places. On this occasion, however, his heart simply wasn't in it. When the Comp were defending a corner early in the second half, he stood idly in the centre-circle with Gregg, their presence at least obliging Grimthorpe to keep players back to cover them.

'Are you OK, Luke?' asked Gregg. 'I mean, you're not even droning on as usual. What's the matter?'

'It's the cabin,' he murmured. 'It's been a bit of a shock.'

'Yeah, right. Do you think we'll still be able to play tomorrow?'

'Only if we can get hold of some nets in time.'

Gregg thought for a moment, watching Tubs slice the ball out for yet another corner. 'What about Frosty?' he suggested. 'You could ask him if we might borrow some from the school.'

'He'd never let us do that.'

Gregg gave a shrug. 'No harm in asking. He can only say no.'

'Yeah, and that's exactly what he'd delight in doing as well. Bet he wouldn't even give me the mud off his boots.'

'Perhaps if you caught him in a good mood?'

Luke gave a snort. 'No chance! Have *you* ever seen Frosty in a good mood? And he sure won't be today, getting stuffed in the Final.'

'Wake up, you dozy pair!'

The Comp's new strike force were so busy talking, they didn't realize the ball had been booted away until Frosty's bellow stirred them into belated action. Gregg managed to get in a challenge, blocking the attempted clearance, and the ball spun across to Luke. He shaped to knock a pass back to Jon, but made no contact and the ball slithered through his legs.

It was a perfect dummy! His marker was completely fooled, thrown off-balance, and was unable to stop the ball running free towards the wing. Brain had sprinted upfield and found himself with a clear route to goal.

The Grimthorpe keeper came out to meet the winger in the vain hope of forcing an error, but with Brain's two-footed ball-skills, there would only be one winner in this type of situation. Brain waltzed round the stranded goalie and tucked the ball into the empty net before dribbling it back to the centre-circle so as not to delay the restart.

'Magic, Brain!' Jon congratulated the scorer. 'We're only one goal behind now. We can still win this.'

Brain grinned. 'You're starting to sound like Luke.'

'Sorry, must be 'cos I'm captain,' Jon said sheepishly. 'Didn't used to care much who won so long as it was a good game.'

'I'll let you off. It *is* the Final after all. Wouldn't mind winning the Cup myself.'

'OK, then – let's do it!'

# 8  The Swinging Pendulum

'C'mon, Reds!' cried the Grimthorpe teacher. 'Sort it out!'

His players were slow to recognize the danger signs of the Comp's revival. If the Reds had been assuming they already had one hand on the trophy, their grip was first loosened and then prized off altogether.

The Comp went close to levelling the scores twice before Brain moved smoothly on to Jon's pin-point pass and slid the ball underneath the goalie's dive for the equalizer. Jon and Brain were the team's genuine stars, capable – when on song – of forcing any opponents to dance to their tune.

'Great stuff!' cried Luke, pushing his worries to the back of his mind during the goal celebrations. 'We've got 'em on the run!'

Frosty was astonished by such a recovery. He had given the game up as dead at half-time. 'Keep it up!' he called out. 'You can win this.'

The players already knew that. Only rarely now did the ball come Sanjay's way and stir the keeper into action. He comfortably held on to a hopeful, long-range effort and then had to deal with a back-pass from Big Ben. He picked the ball up and prepared to boot it as far as he could . . .

When the whistle blew, Sanjay thought it was the signal for the end of the match and he belted the ball high into the air instead. Only then did he realize that something was wrong – terribly wrong. He was helped to arrive at this conclusion by all the abuse he was receiving from his teammates.

'Handball!' announced the referee. 'Free-kick to the Reds.'

'You idiot, Sanjay!' cried Gary. 'What did you go and do a stupid thing like that for? You know you can't handle the ball from a back-pass!'

Sanjay shook his head in dismay. 'Soz – I just wasn't thinking, like . . .'

His voice trailed away. The Comp players were in no mood for explanations or apologies.

'Make a wall!' ordered Jon.

Luke was about to join it when his cousin grabbed him by the arm. 'You go upfield, Luke,' Jon urged. 'We need a target man in case we make a quick breakaway.'

'Good thinking, Johan,' grinned Luke. It didn't cross his mind that Jon might simply want him out of the way.

Luke's presence didn't cause the Reds any particular concern. 'I'll look after this clown,' announced the centre-back, waving his fellow defenders forward to join the attack. 'He's no bother.'

Luke ignored the comment and gave the unemployed commentator his job back. *'Here we*

*are, right near the end of the Cup Final, and the Comp have some desperate defending to do. The human wall prepares to risk life and limb to block this free-kick as it looks like it's gonna be a real blaster. The kicker runs in and lets fly . . . Oh! That must have hurt Tubs, the biggest brick in the wall. And now the ball's been hoofed clear and . . .'*

'Luke!' came Jon's cry, cutting across the commentary. 'Chase it!'

Luke jolted into belated action. He scurried after the ball and managed to reach it just ahead of the slow-moving opponent, receiving a kick on the ankle as his reward. He stumbled and lost what little control he had over the ball, but as his marker was about to hammer it back into the Comp's half, Luke stretched out a leg and toe-poked it away. The defender whacked into Luke's foot instead and the pair of them collapsed to the ground in pain.

Luke didn't even see the goal, preventing any live commentary on how Jon gained possession of the loose ball and then lobbed it calmly over the keeper's head. The first Luke knew about what had happened was when he was suddenly hauled to his feet and nearly deafened.

'4–3!' Gregg shrieked into his ear. 'We've won the Cup!'

\*

'So where did you get the nets?' asked Big Ben.

'From the Comp,' Luke replied, watching his dad and uncle fasten the nets on to the goalposts at the far end of the recreation ground.

'Did you go and pinch 'em or something?'

'Course not. Just asked Frosty if the Swifts could borrow some nets for our last league match and he said yes. Even lent us a couple of footballs.'

'Amazing!' Big Ben chuckled. 'Perhaps he *is* human after all!'

'Well, we *had* just won the cup for him,' said Luke, fingering the medal that still hung around his neck on a coloured ribbon. It was the first medal Luke had ever received. Not just at football, but for anything.

He was feeling a great sense of relief now, knowing that he wasn't to blame for the cabin fire. When the footballers returned to Swillsby after the Final, they learnt that the arsonists had also damaged several other buildings, including a barn, part of the village hall and the old scout hut.

'Er, just one more thing, Skipper,' said Big Ben, grinning. 'Are you gonna be wearing that all match?'

'What?'

'That medal. Bet you even slept with it round your neck!'

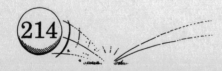

214

'Course not,' Luke replied, reddening. 'What d'yer think I am?'

The defender didn't like to say. Nor did he see Luke slip the medal inside his soccer shirt out of sight as more of the team began to arrive.

'Just for safe keeping,' Luke told himself. 'I mean, can't leave it lying around anywhere, can I? Somebody might nick it.'

The players stood about at first, not knowing quite what to do in the absence of the cabin.

'So where are we gonna change?' asked Sean.

'Alfresco,' said Luke.

'Where's that?'

'Here.'

'Where?'

'It means outside,' Luke explained. 'Ricki told me it comes from the Italian originally.'

'Pity he had to go back to Italy himself today,' muttered Tubs. 'We needed him here.'

Sean wouldn't let the matter drop. 'You mean, we've all got to strip off in the open where everybody can see us?'

'Everybody!' Titch cackled, looking around comically at the otherwise deserted recky. 'Don't seem as if the prospect of watching us lot parading around in our Y-fronts has drawn much of a crowd!'

'The Rangers won't like it,' Sean muttered, taking off his coat.

'Well, they'll just have to lump it, won't they?' said Luke, losing his patience. 'What else can we do?'

'Shame it's not foggy like last time,' put in Mark. 'Even Tubs could have streaked across the pitch then and nobody would have noticed!'

The Swifts' previous attempt to play this fixture against Padley Park Rangers had been abandoned in the fog with the game officially goal-less, despite Luke's claims that he'd scored just before the referee called a halt. The visibility by that time was so poor that not even the

Rangers keeper saw him put the ball in the net.

Sean was correct about one thing. The visitors certainly didn't think much of the situation when they eventually rolled up and had to change, grumbling, in the car park.

'Right, men – all ready?' cried Luke to get his teammates attention. Nobody responded to his usual rallying call, but he carried on regardless. 'One last big effort today and the Swifts will be safe.'

'Are you sure about that, Skipper?' said Titch. 'I mean, we ain't got many points this season.'

'Nor have the Wanderers. So long as we win today, we'll be OK.'

'What if we don't?'

'Look, like I've told you, it's between us and Wanderers who goes down – right?' Luke explained, deciding to spell out the situation again. 'We're both playing our last game today and we're one point ahead of them. So if we pick up the three points for a win, they can't catch us.'

'But what if we don't?' Titch persisted, repeating his question.

'Well, in that case, it'll depend how they get on, won't it?'

'And how we gonna know that? They gonna show the results on the telly, are they?'

'No need. Dad's got a mobile phone.'

'So?'

'And so has Uncle Ray.'

'Fat lot of good that is,' chortled Tubs, gazing over at the two men who had just finished dealing with the nets. 'May as well save the cost of a call. They're standing next to each other.'

Luke pulled a face. 'They won't be in a bit. Ray's taking Johan to watch the Wanderers game and they're going to ring to let us know what's happening.'

'Ah, the wonders of modern technology!' put in Big Ben sarcastically. 'I trust they know how to work the things.'

'Course they do,' Luke scoffed, trying to hide his own doubts.'

Ray saw the first goal go in even before he left the recky, but it didn't send him off in an optimistic mood. It was scored by the Rangers.

For once, it was not due to any mistake of Luke's, or even Sanjay's. It was simply a very good goal, rounding off a move that would have tested the best defence in the league – and that was something the Swifts certainly could not boast.

Their *goals against* tally almost needed a separate column in the league table, the number

was so big. It was no use them hoping to stay up on *goal difference*. If they finished level on points with Wanderers, the Swifts were doomed for relegation into the new bottom division that was being formed for all the clubs wanting to join the league next season.

The Rangers kept Sanjay very busy for the next quarter of an hour, but they only succeeded in playing the unpredictable goalie into form. He produced a series of excellent saves, the best being a spectacular leap to pluck the ball out of the air. He even clung on to it as he hit the ground.

By contrast, the Rangers keeper had been largely idle and he was caught napping by a surprise Swifts raid up the right wing. Dazza's speed took him past a defender and his centre-cum-shot found the keeper out of position. The boy's blushes were only spared when the ball dipped a fraction too late and clipped the top of the crossbar on its way out for a goal-kick.

That should have served as a sufficient wake-up alarm call, but when Brain broke through a few minutes later, the keeper was again in no-man's-land. Brain's cross sailed over his head and dropped perfectly on to Gregg's. Even then, Gregg almost steered the ball wide of the target,

220

but it snicked the inside of the post and deflected into the netting.

'The equalizer!' cried Luke, rushing over to congratulate both the scorer and the provider. 'There's no stopping us now.'

# 9 Keep in Touch

The phone rang almost as soon as the Swifts gathered together at half-time. Luke's dad jabbed at a button and put the mobile to his ear.

'Hello,' he said. 'Who's that?'

*'It's me, you fool,'* came his brother's response. *'Who d'yer think?'*

'Oh, right, sorry – so what's the news?'

*'Bad. Wanderers went 2–1 in front just before the break. What about the Swifts?'*

'Better. Everything still to play for here. Gregg's just equalized. What shall I tell the kids?'

*'Tell them the truth,'* said Ray. *'No good trying to mislead them, that's only asking for trouble.'*

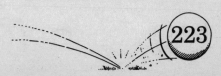

'Right, OK, leave it to me.'

Dad switched off and faced a clamour of voices wanting to know what was happening in the other game.

'C'mon, Dad – don't keep us in suspense,' Luke pleaded.

Dad made an instant decision to apply a bit of amateur psychology. 'Good news,' he announced, forcing a smile to cover his deception. He didn't want the players to be discouraged by the truth. 'Wanderers are losing.'

'Heavily?' Luke said hopefully.

'Er . . . no, just a goal in it at half-time.'

Luke eyed his dad suspiciously. 'So why did you have to ask Ray what to tell us?'

'Well, he said the Wanderers were still looking dangerous, that's all,' Dad replied, a little flustered. 'We can't afford to relax.'

'No way we'll do that,' Luke asserted. 'As long as we win, they won't be able to catch us.'

'Right, you heard your captain, lads,' Dad said. 'Just concentrate on your own job. Win this game and we're safe, it's as simple as that.'

'Huh! Winning's never as simple as that for us,' muttered Big Ben.

'Yeah, but if Wanderers *do* lose, it won't matter if we do, too, will it?' Gary pointed out. 'We'll still be OK.'

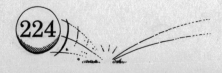

'You can't rely on that,' Dad said quickly. 'Just go and do your best, lads, that's all we can ask of you. Good luck!'

'Reckon we're gonna need it,' muttered Sanjay, watching the animated discussions in the opposing camp thirty metres away. 'Bet they can't work out why they're not already well ahead.'

'It's thanks to you, Sanjay,' Luke chirped, pleased to have the rare chance to praise his goalie. 'Keep playing like that and there's no way they'll get the ball past you again.'

That was asking for trouble. Luke should have known better. Sanjay's form was as changeable

as the weather in an English summer. One minute glorious sunshine, the next a downpour of rain – with always the risk of occasional showers.

Five minutes into the second half, Sanjay dropped the inevitable clanger – and the ball – and his teammates felt like reaching for the shelter of their umbrellas. Having done well to turn the original shot around the post, he let the corner slip through his hands and a lurking striker knocked the loose ball between two defenders on the line to put Rangers back in front.

Dad's phone went once more. It was Jon this time.

*''Fraid Wanderers have scored again,'* he reported. *'They're 3–1 up now. What's the score your end?'*

'Not looking good. We've just gone 2–1 down.'

*'Pity! Well, make sure Luke knows about Wanderers, won't you?'*

'Sure, thanks for telling me.'

Luke came running over. 'Heard the phone. Wanderers haven't equalized, have they?'

Dad shook his head. 'Er . . . no,' he said, attempting an answer which was strictly true, if not exactly accurate. 'Just you keep your mind on the game here, that's the main thing.'

Luke veered away to broadcast the latest news to the world via his commentary and then to his teammates. 'Big effort, men,' he cried, shaking his fists. 'C'mon, we can still do it.'

'Just hope things work out OK,' Dad muttered, 'or I'm in big trouble!'

His hopes were raised a minute later when Brain was gifted a great chance to put the Swifts back on level terms. A Rangers defender turned the ball back towards his keeper without noticing Brain was hovering. The winger reached the ball first and pushed it wide of the onrushing keeper, but unfortunately just wide of the goal too.

Brain stared after it in horror. 'Can't believe I missed that!' he groaned.

Nor could Luke. And nor could he believe the arrival of a most unexpected spectator. 'What's *he* doing here?' he muttered. 'I hope he's not gonna bring us bad luck.'

Frosty wandered up to stand next to Luke's dad. 'Hello again,' the teacher greeted him. 'What's the damage?'

'Damage?' repeated Dad, as much taken aback as the players. 'Er . . . to the cabin, you mean?'

Frosty gazed over to the charred wreckage. It made a sorry sight. 'No, I can see that for myself,' he replied. 'I meant, how many are your Swifts losing by today?'

'Oh, sorry. Well, not doing badly, I suppose – only 2–1 down, but we really need to win.'

'So I gather – bit much to hope for, isn't it?'

Dad took offence. 'Well, they managed it for you yesterday.'

Frosty nodded slowly. 'Aye, they did that,' he acknowledged, but couldn't resist a little dig. 'Shame Jon can't turn out for you as well, though.'

'He's doing his bit – keeping us in touch with the other vital game . . .'

The phone rang again at that moment.

'Excuse me,' Dad said, clamping it to his ear.

229

Jon relayed his report and Dad muttered a brief response, not wishing to become involved in any long explanation with Frosty nearby.

'So what's the situation there, then?' Frosty asked.

Dad hesitated, but he couldn't bring himself to lie to the teacher as well. 'Wanderers have just let a goal in, but they're still winning unfortunately . . .'

'Do these lads know that?'

'Well, you see, actually I was . . .'

Frosty took matters into his own hands. 'C'mon, you Swifts, pull your fingers out!' he roared. 'No good losing when the other lot are winning.'

The Swifts glanced at one another, startled. 'What's he mean, they're winning?' muttered Big Ben. 'Can't be.'

'Must have hit back second half,' groaned Mark. 'We're dead!'

Luke ran towards the touchline in alarm. 'What's going on, Dad?' he gasped. 'Tell me.'

'Sorry – Wanderers are 3–2 up,' he admitted reluctantly.

Luke's world caved in. He knew that even a draw wouldn't be enough to save the Swifts now, not if the Wanderers picked up all three points. Instinctively, he put his hand inside his shirt

and clasped his medal for comfort. It seemed to inspire him.

'C'mon, men!' he called out, trying to sound positive when he was choked with negative emotions. 'We need to score some goals.'

That was easier said than done. But if cousin Jon couldn't come to the Swifts rescue, then perhaps cousin Ricki would suffice.

'Hey! Look who's here!' cried Gary, pointing at the car park. 'Thought he was flying off to Italy today.'

Ricki galloped towards the pitch. 'Car broke down again,' he shouted out. 'We miss plane.'

'How did you get here?' Luke demanded.

'Laura – her father bring me,' he panted, pulling his boots out of a bag. 'You need me?'

'Sure do,' Luke admitted. 'We have plenty need of you – get 'em on!'

The player-manager decided to gamble by taking off a defender and playing Ricki up front as another attacker. His sweeper role was forgotten.

'Give him your shirt, Mark,' Luke said. 'We don't have a spare one.'

Mark pulled a face. 'So long as he doesn't have to wear my shorts as well. I'm not standing on the recky in my pants.'

'So this is that Ricki kid I've heard about, is it?'

mused Frosty, stroking his stubbly chin. 'Should be interesting to see which Crawford he takes after.'

Ricki's first touch certainly bore the family trademark, but of the Luke variety, ballooning a pass over Brain's head out of play. His second, however, showed he had the potential class of Jon about him as well. He caught the ball on the volley, about knee high, and sent it swerving only centimetres over the Rangers crossbar.

'Hmm, strange combination,' Frosty murmured. 'Got a bit of both in him by the look of it. What a crazy mixed-up kid!'

'Come on, Ricki!' cried Laura. 'Come on the Swifts. You can do it.'

Perhaps Laura had brought them a touch of Lady Luck. In their very next attack, the ball fell at the feet of Ricki in the penalty area. His first effort, a left-foot scoop, was blocked, but he seized on the rebound and hit a right-footed rocket straight at the keeper who parried the ball away to save his teeth. A goalmouth scramble ensued with the ball ricocheting between the bodies until a thin leg poked out of the crush and scuffed it over the line.

Controversy reigned. As the referee signalled a goal, the visitors were appealing for a foul – any kind of foul – claiming pushing, kicking and

shirt-pulling all at once, but the Swifts were much too busy celebrating to notice. Only when the party broke up did it become clear who was claiming the credit as the scorer.

'That's m'boy!' Dad yelled. 'You've shown 'em how to do it!'

Unfortunately, Luke was not able to manage a repeat demonstration. The Rangers decided to settle for a draw and, in the end, the Swifts had to be satisfied with a single point too.

*'That's it, there goes the final whistle,'* sighed the commentator, still in a bit of a daze after the thrill of scoring. *'Not even the skipper's scrambled equalizer may be enough to save his team. As I hand you back to the studio, their fate now hangs in the balance . . .'*

He had to stop talking. His path was barred by the Rangers captain. 'You lot were dead jammy,' the boy sneered. 'We should have thrashed you.'

Luke gave a shrug. He couldn't be bothered to argue. He had more important things on his mind, like the Wanderers result. If their rivals had won, the Swifts would be relegated.

Dad was messing with the mobile as Luke approached, trying to get through to Ray without success.

'Here, let me have a go,' Luke said, holding out his hand impatiently.

As Dad tossed him the phone in frustration, it jangled into life and Luke nearly dropped it into the water bucket. He put it shakily to his ear as his teammates crowded around, expecting to hear the worst.

'Hello, it's Luke here. We drew two each. What's gone on there?'

The audience craned forward, hoping to catch a few words, but all they could hear was a crackle on the line.

'Soz, I didn't catch that, Johan,' said Luke. 'Got some interference. Say again . . . who scored?'

After a few more crackles, Luke suddenly flung the phone up into the air and Dad went scampering after it.

'We've done it!' Luke cried at the top of his voice. 'We're safe!'

The Swifts cheered and jumped all over each other in relief, and it was some while before anyone calmed down enough to ask a sensible question.

'So what exactly went on there, Skipper?' said a half-naked Titch, who had somehow lost his shirt in all the excitement.

'The Wanderers screwed up!' Luke exclaimed.

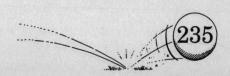

'Johan said they panicked and threw it away.'

'Just like you did with my phone,' Dad grumbled, giving it a shake.

'What was the score?' Tubs demanded.

'Same as our Cup Final – 4–3! Wanderers went and let in two goals in the last few minutes of the game. They must be pig-sick!'

Luke himself felt totally overcome, mentally and physically drained of emotion. He went to sit on the blackened steps of the burnt-out cabin and let his automatic commentary describe the scene. The visitors were trailing moodily back to the car park, Frosty had already started to

dismantle one of the nets, their Latin Romeo was giving Laura a hug right in front of her father and his dishevelled, delirious teammates were still behaving like lunatics.

*'Even after all the recent shocks, the biggest must be that – for once – things have actually worked out right for the Swifts,'* Luke murmured as a final summary. *'And you can bet your life that this crazy bunch of unsung heroes will want to do it all over again next season too! Soccer mad, all of 'em – Luke Crawford's Barmy Army!'*

# Crawford's Corner

Hi! It's me again, Luke Crawford – still on a high after skippering the Swifts to our dramatic end of season success. Well, at least we didn't finish bottom of the table and that's as good a reason as any to celebrate. Not to mention helping to win the cup for old Frosty in his final year at the Comp of course. Oops! I've just gone and mentioned it.

Was originally thinking of telling you here about a few soccer shocks of the past to go with the title of this book. Like, for instance, when the part-time footballers of the United States beat favourites England 1–0 during the 1950 World Cup – or when an on-loan goalkeeper went upfield for a corner in the dying seconds of a game in 1999 to score the vital goal that saved Carlisle being relegated from the Football League – or even when a referee last dared to give a penalty against Manchester United at Old Trafford!

But I'm too excited right now to go trawling through all my collection of soccer annuals to dig out more examples of such fascinating feats. If you've got time, why don't you do some research of your own into the record books and read about all the amazing things that have happened over the years on the football field? Use the Internet, too, and see what else you can find out.

Instead, I've decided to return to my favourite subject – the legendary superstar, **Johan Cruyff**, known to friends as Jopie, and nicknamed **the Flying Dutchman**. Unbelievably, I still sometimes get blank looks from other kids when I rave on about how great a player he was, the best ever as far as I'm concerned – better even than Pelé. You'd have thought they'd never heard of him! Yeah, OK, I know Johan graced the scene well before our time, but footballers only have short careers at the top. The players you rate now will soon be history.

But what a fabulous history Johan Cruyff has, though, both as a world-famous star player and as a successful coach. In my view, there's no-one to equal his achievements, even though he never managed to win the World Cup. The closest he came to that was as captain of the brilliant Dutch

team which lost 2–1 in the 1974 Final to West Germany. This was despite their exciting style of play, known as *Total Football*, where all the versatile Dutch players constantly switched positions during games.

Speaking of the Net, by the way, there are hundreds of sites on the subject of Johan Cruyff, even if some of them are in Dutch and other languages! (His name rhymes with either *life* or *roof*, whichever you prefer.) Browse through that lot and you'll know nearly as much as I do about his fantastic career. To start you off, here's a potted biography of his life and honours:

- born Hendrik Johannes Cruyff on 25 April 1947 in Amsterdam
- family lived across the street from Ajax stadium
- started playing for Ajax Juniors at age of ten
- won his first cup when he was 14 and played all his later career with that trademark number 14 on the back of his shirt
- 1964 – scored on first team debut for Ajax at 16
- 1966 – scored last-minute equalizer in 2–2 draw on debut for Holland

- won three successive European Cups with Ajax – 1971/72/73
- 1973 – transferred to Barcelona for a then record fee of £922,000
- 1974 – birth of son Jordi, later to play also for Ajax, Barcelona and then Manchester United
- won ten league championship medals:
  Ajax – 1966/67/68/70/72/73/82/83
  Barcelona – 1974 (their first for 14 years in his first season there)
  Feyenoord – 1984
- won seven cup-winners medals:
  Ajax – 1967/70/71/72/83
  Barcelona – 1978
  Feyenoord – 1984
- voted European Footballer of the Year in 1971, 1973 & 1974
- voted best European Footballer of the Century in 1999
- retired from international football in 1977 before the '78 World Cup
- played a couple of years in America before returning to Ajax in 1981
- hung up his boots in 1984 after season with rivals Feyenoord

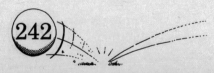

- Ajax technical director, trainer & coach from 1985 to 1988
- Barcelona coach from 1988 to 1996
- main honours as coach:

  League Championships: Barcelona –
  1991/92/93/94

  Cups:  Ajax – 1986/87

  Barcelona – 1990

  European Cup: Barcelona – 1992

  European Cup-Winners Cups:

  Ajax – 1987

  Barcelona – 1989
- Fired as Barcelona coach in 1996 after dispute with club president
- Celebrated his 50th birthday in 1997 in semi-retirement, but set up the Johan Cruyff Foundation to raise money to help disabled people play sport. Now fully recovered from his earlier heart problems, due to heavy smoking, he may yet be back. Watch this space!

Phew! A record like that, both as player and coach, would take some beating, eh? To repeat what I put in *Soccer Stars* when I was writing about lots of great players, I described Johan Cruyff as the

complete footballer. He had everything: pace, acceleration, instant ball control, amazing balance and superb passing skills – and he also scored loads of goals (netting 33 times in his 48 internationals). He was such an elegant player, so versatile and original, even inventing a new ingenious piece of dribbling trickery which became known as the 'Cruyff Turn'. You must have seen it shown on TV – but I bet you can't do it! (No, neither can I, sadly.)

I don't want to make out that Johan was a saint of course. Far from it. He was quite a controversial figure, on and off the field. He knew exactly what he wanted and was always prepared to argue his case. He was even booked at half-time in the 1974 World Cup Final for questioning the referee about his decisions as they left the pitch! He was also the first Dutch player to be sent off in an international and received a year's ban!

Some people might have viewed him as arrogant at times, but not by those who really knew him. He had to put up with a lot of rough treatment in matches, and did so with dignity and self-control, even though many defenders weren't quick enough to foul him. Before they realized what he was going to do, he'd done it and whipped past them. He had

tremendous speed off the mark and was able to do things naturally that most other players could never do after years of practice. That's what made him so special. He may have been frail looking, but he had great stamina, technique and tactical knowledge. He worked hard to overcome any weaknesses in his game, building up the power in his left foot, for example, by training with weights on his ankle in his teens to develop more strength so that he could kick a ball equally hard with both feet.

As a coach, he stressed what he had always believed as a player – that simple play is the most beautiful, and that you should try and play in an attacking style to make the game a more enjoyable spectacle to watch. He once said that if a team is 4–0 ahead near the end of a match, it's better for the next shot to hit the woodwork rather than go in so the crowd could 'oooh' and 'aaah' in excitement.

Football, he insisted, is a game you play with your brains. There's no need to run around so much. You just have to be in the right place at the right time, not too early, not too late. (Tubs would obviously agree with him there – trouble is, Tubs can't run even if he wanted to and he hasn't got

many brains either! Only joking, Tubs, my old mate, if you happen to read this.)

Right, so there you are. Better stop or I'll go on all day and I'm getting hungry. But now you know why Johan Cruyff was such a magnificent footballer and top class coach. No excuse any more to say 'Who?' when you hear his name. He WAS and ALWAYS WILL BE the GREATEST! 'That's logical,' as J.C. himself often liked to say to clinch an argument.

See ya!

*Luke*

# ABOUT THE AUTHOR

Rob Childs was born and grew up in Derby. His childhood ambition was to become an England cricketer or footballer – preferably both! After university, however, he went into teaching and taught in primary and high schools in Leicestershire, where he now lives. Always interested in school sports, he coached school teams and clubs across a range of sports, and ran area representative teams in football, cricket and athletics.

Recognizing a need for sports fiction for young readers, he decided to have a go at writing such stories himself and now has more than fifty books to his name, including the popular *The Big Match* series, published by Young Corgi Books and the *County Cup* series.

Rob has now left teaching in order to be able to write full-time. Married to Joy, a writer herself, Rob is also a keen photographer, providing many pictures for Joy's books and articles

# SOCCER MAD DOUBLE

Includes FOOTBALL DAFT
and FOOTBALL FLUKES

## FOOTBALL DAFT
Brian Draper – known as Brain – is
the Swifts' top goalscorer. But why won't
he try out for the school team?

## FOOTBALL FLUKES
Giantkillers? Luke is determined to
show everyone that the Swift's first-round
victory in the cup wasn't simply a fluke...

0440 864488
Corgi Yearling Books

# THE BIG CUP COLLECTION

Can Danebridge lift the Cup?

## THE BIG CLASH
Chris Weston is under a lot of pressure as
captain and goalie of Danebridge School
football team. With the team battling to avoid
relegation, Chris needs to be on top form to
keep their hopes alive in the cup...

## THE BIG DROP
Danebridge need to pull together to
gain the vital points they need from their last
few matches of the season. But then bully-boy
Luke Bradshaw gets their leading goalscorer
into serious trouble...

## THE BIG SEND-OFF
Danebridge face a crucial semi-final replay –
a match they must win if they are to meet
their arch-rivals, Shenby, in the Final...

0552 547646
Young Corgi Books

## THE BIG FOOTBALL COLLECTION

Football! A great game – best in the world!

### THE BIG GAME
Keen young footballer Andrew Weston
is sure that his skills in defence will help
the school team win every match. Until he
discovers who their first opponents are...

### THE BIG MATCH
A dream comes true for Chris Weston when
he is picked to stand in for the school team's
regular goalkeeper for a vital cup game.

### THE BIG PRIZE
Chris Weston is going to be the mascot for
the local football league club for their next
F.A. Cup match! Then disaster strikes...

Three fast-moving and realistic stories
from a popular series about two
football-mad brothers.

0552 542970
Young Corgi Books

# THE BIG FOOTBALL FRENZY

A super treble of action-packed football!

## THE BIG WIN

Midfielder Mark Towers has just struck
lucky: his family has won the Lottery!  But
Chris Weston, captain of Danebridge School
football team, wants a different kind of
big win – on the football pitch…

## THE BIG FIX

A new season and a new team for captain
Chris.  But can Danebridge win against their
arch-rivals, Shenby, when the referee seems
to be playing against them too?

## THE BIG FREEZE

Chris captains the team in an exciting
triangular tournament – on the unfamiliar
surface of an all-weather pitch!

'All the excitement and fervour
the fans expect… splendid'
BOOKS FOR KEEPS

0552 547026
Young Corgi Books